TERROR
COLOR CODE RED

SCOTT PLUMMER

ISBN 978-1-956010-06-0 (paperback)
ISBN 978-1-956010-07-7 (digital)

Rushmore Press LLC
1 800 460 9188
www.rushmorepress.com

Printed in the United States of America

I'd like to dedicate this book to my muse and inspiration
Dr. Tammy Stevens, the kindest woman I have ever known
and whom I based the April Gellar character on.

CHAPTER ONE

KABUL AFGHANISTAN FOUR YEARS AGO

It was the twenty-sixth of September in Kabul. Summer had just finished days earlier, but it was still unbelievably hot. The frigid temperatures of the afghan winter would soon be upon us.

I was scheduled to fly home in less than a month. Full of apprehensions because in the last few letters from home my wife seemed a little distant. I figured I was imagining things but still I wouldn't relax until I got home.

Things in the capital had been relatively quiet now for the last couple of months. The real worries came when you were assigned to patrol the east or northeast sections of the country.

I was on my way back to base camp for the day when I came upon two British officers who were lighting up a smoke, on the other side of the street. It was still too early to arrive back at camp, so I thought I'd be sociable and walk over and say hello to the British. Halfway across the street, I noticed an elderly local man pushing his hand cart full of groceries past the British soldiers. Then a feeling came over me and I was on my back, lying on the road. My teeth felt like an electrical current was continuously circling through them.

My nose was bleeding and all I could hear was a high-pitched whistle, ringing in my ears. The ground around me that was dry and dusty just a moment earlier was now thick drenched mud. It took me a minute to realize the mud was not made up of the traditional dirt and water but instead it was a combination of dirt and blood. At first, I thought it was my blood, and then when I spotted a bodiless arm lying about a foot to my right, a sickening panic overtook me. Then when I struggled to survey around me, I spotted a leg lying to my left with an army boot on the foot. I was still dazed and confused as I tried to move my arms and legs. My right arm and leg I could see movement, but my left arm and leg I saw nothing. I was now convinced that I had found the owner of the bodiless limbs, and to my chagrin it was me.

I don't know how long I was lying on the ground but just that panic and thirst were drowning my entire being. Then mercifully the entire sun was blacked out from in front of me by a giant of a man, who was yelling something at me. I could see his mouth moving but couldn't understand a single thing he said because the ringing in my ears was too loud. Suddenly I felt my body rising up and a strange floating sensation overtook me only to be painfully interrupted by a knifing pain in my lower back. My hearing started to return as the piercing whistling noise started to subside. I glanced around at my surroundings and the first thing I noticed was the old man pushing the cart's headless body was lying beside his burning cart. Then I saw my two British colleagues who were only distinguishable by the uniforms left on their limbless torsos.

My friendly medic smiled at me, he had a massive head and was missing a few front teeth. As my medic spoke it became evident from his strong accent that he was Australian. "You're going to be all right Angus; we are just going to take you to the hospital. You have all your parts still on. There's a piece of metal stuck in your lower left back, but we'll wait until the hospital to let the doctors remove it."

I must have passed out on the way to the hospital because the next thing I remember was bright lights and lots of noise. I was on a stretcher being wheeled into a room where there were even more people and noise. My confusion had totally engulfed me. It seemed like all the voices were talking to me all at once. I couldn't focus in on anyone's voice. I strained my ears and was finally able to concentrate on one voice. I t was my nurses, a middle-aged heavy-set woman. She was a black woman with a big round face; her hair was a mixture of black and grey. But the most fixating feature she had was the enormous compassion in her big dark eyes. I felt instantly safe with this woman. I asked for some water to rid the taste of the desert from inside my mouth. My nurse feeds it to me gently through a straw, making me take small sips for me not to choke on the water. After there was some relief to my thirst I decided to take inventory of my body. I was able to lift my right arm up to my face and move all my fingers, well. Then I lifted my right leg, it rose but a knife-like pain shot through my lower back. After relaxing my leg, I checked my left side, I moved my arm, but it must have been strapped down because nothing happened. Then my left leg, I tried to lift but again nothing other than the unwelcome return of my knifing back pain.

"Angus the orderly is going to take you to the operating room now to remove that nasty piece of metal from your back. You will be back here before you know what happened, okay darling?" said my delightful nurse.

I was back in my bed, but the pain was unbelievable. My nurse with a big smile holding a needle said, "Okay let's get rid of that nasty pain." She injected the fluid into my I-V tube. The effect was almost immediate as my head felt a wave of utopia sweep over it. My pain was now just a memory as I fell into a light sleep.

When I awoke, I was sailing on a beautiful summer day in the middle of Lake Huron surrounded by friends. The cool lake breeze felt so refreshing. Then suddenly a sharp prick in my hand sends me speeding back to my hospital bed in Kabul. When my mind finally returns to normality, I see the doctor standing beside my bed looking at my chart. My doc was a crusty man in his fifties with a badly receding hairline. The rest of his hair was white. His face was stern, probably from seeing far too many trauma cases. His demeanor was not that of the ideal bedside manner. He placed the chart in front of his face so that he could read it while he talked. It also helped him prevent eye contact.

"Angus we just got back your results from your c t scan and it seems the blast in the market caused a blood vessel in your brain to explode. You will have to stay in the trauma unit for a few more days."

Later that day at least I think it was still the same day my commanding officer and best friend in Afghanistan John Gagnon came by to visit me. John is a great man and leader. He is from Quebec City and has been a lifer in anti-terror and now the army. He stands at 5'9" with perfect posture. He weighs a strong 175pounds. He has a great sense of humor and knows exactly how to let his subordinates relax, without ever letting them lose discipline or stop being cautious. John had recently been made the commander of all allied troops in Kabul.

"What's wrong Angus? Couldn't you wait the rest of the month to be sent on leave?" Not in a joking mood, I drift off to sleep again, as the drugs take back their grip on my reality.

This time I awake to great confusion with a nurse straddling my chest yelling "Angus, Angus, breath, breath." I again fall under again this time to wake in a new section, hooked up to machines that are buzzing and clicking. I survey the area and count three units of blood dripping into my arm. There are two more bags of clear liquid dripping into a tube that is stuck into my neck. There are also two tubes stuck up my nose, one in each nostril leading to who knows where. The discomfort is almost unbearable but at least the sharp pain in my back has subsided.

It's a few hours or days later and my doctor has returned to see me "It looks like you are out of the woods now Angus." so I ask "Does that mean I should be back on my feet soon?"

"God no, I meant that you are going to live. Your chances of ever walking again are pretty well zero. "Adds my friendly supportive doctor.

I try to remember that cheery little speech every time I am told that I can't accomplish something because now I can perform at levels equal or close to what I was like before the blast. I have been given medical leave from my position with Canada's elite anti-terrorist squad the elite Joint Task Force two.

On my arrival to Toronto, my best friend from high school is waiting for me. It is a pleasant surprise to see Jim Williams Jim played defensive end on our high school football team. He still is an imposing figure at 6'4" 250 pounds. Jim says" Angus as soon as you fell up to it, I could use another salesman at Ideal plumbing supplies

After three years of intense therapy, I decided to take Jim up on his offer.

CHAPTER TWO

CAIRO EGYPT CURRENT YEAR

In a Cairo hotel room, Elisa Levi pretending she is on vacation is really monitoring the web searching for possible terrorist messages while working for the Israeli Massoud. In school, nobody ever would have guessed that Elisa was to become a spy but her natural knowledge of computers and her mastery of eight languages made her a natural to surf the net looking for clues. Elisa usually does her work from her homeland but an unusual amount of traffic on the net has inspired her bosses to give Elisa her first road assignment. So, Elisa packs up and heads off to a resort in Egypt under the guise that she is a German computer technician on holidays for a three-week stint. Elisa's soft feminine features and her lack of an aura of confidence led her superiors to believe Elisa wouldn't be suspected of being a spy during her three-week assignment.

In her second week at the resort other than the odd trip to the pool or to the resort restaurant and coffee shop, Elisa has spent the whole time in her room working hoping to find something to reward her bosses in the faith that they bestowed upon her. On the Tuesday of the second week, Elisa returned to her room surprised to find that she had forgotten to turn her computer off. Her heart flips for a second then she looks around the room and everything is just as she left it. Elisa realizes that she is just being paranoid, so she shuts off her computer and heads back to the pool for an hour of sun.

Back at the pool, Elisa is struck by the looks of a thirty-something Italian man, who has jet black medium-length curly hair. She is especially fond of his six-pack abs. Elisa has now forgotten her paranoid scare completely as she sits and is captivated by her Italian man's movements. Two hours later the man makes eye contact with Elisa and smiles as he dries his hair. Elisa looks away quickly and feels the blood rushing to her cheeks in embarrassment. The young Italian man grabs his things and walks away put he pauses to glance back and smile at Elisa again. In her state of embarrassment, Elisa notices that she has been at the pool for three hours, so she grabs her bag and towel and heads back to her room to work.

Back in her room Elisa flips on her machine and starts to search the known sites of Islamic radical propaganda. Elisa struggles to get the hard body of her Italian man out of her head when she stumbles across a new site that she finds intriguing. In it, there is a tall man speaking Arabic wearing a black robe covering him from head to toe. His message is "My fellow brothers of the great intifada, our time draws near. Victory will soon be ours. Our enemies will soon suffer the greatest defeat in their short history. It will be a victory of epic proportions. The ground they walk on will shake from below with Allah's fury. The great Satan will crumble to his knees like the true cowards that they are. Thus, ending their support for the Zionist pigs. This spring will be the beginning of our greatest victory and our first attack on our enemies' soil since September of two thousand and one. All my brothers and sisters, now is the time to join our cause and fight alongside Allah."

Elisa flushed with excitement immediately e-mails her superiors back home.

Elisa pleased with her days' work decides that tonight she will head out to a disco that specializes in entertaining western guests. Elisa excitedly gets dressed, putting on her tight grey dress that clings to her shapely body. The dress is short hemmed a good 10 inches above her knees. Elisa is a tall thin shapely woman standing five foot nine and weighing only one hundred and twenty well-proportioned pounds. For a thin woman, Elisa has a rather large chest. Her dress is low cut revealing an ample amount of cleavage. Elisa puts on her make up then views herself in the full-length mirror, Elisa is quite proud of the way she looks. She can't help but gloat wondering what her classmates would think of her now, a shapely successful woman leading the exciting life of a spy.

The club is only two blocks away, so Elisa decides to walk to the club on this beautiful clear night. Elisa has great difficulty walking to the club due to her three-and-a-half-inch spiked heels. Elisa knew she would have trouble with her shoes because she hardly ever wears heels, but she couldn't resist the way her long legs looked so good in her black shoes.

Elisa arrives at the club and is nervous about her first night out since her arrival. Inside the club is only half full because it is only ten o'clock. Elisa gazes around first to the huge dance floor that has its own light show directed on it, then to the two-sided bar that is at least one hundred yards long. Elisa decides it's the bar where she will sit and have a drink first. Elisa sits down in the middle in a spot where there are at least four empty stools on each side of her. She orders a glass of white wine and is immediately disappointed that she didn't order something more exotic.

Elisa sits sipping her wine nervously wondering how long she will sit alone or how long she will stay. She doesn't have to contemplate too long for her thoughts are interrupted by a tap on her shoulder. Elisa turns to look and her heart jumps as she is face to face staring into the big dark eyes of her Italian gentleman from the pool. He asks "May I buy you a drink?" Elisa almost says no thank you, I have one, but she glances at her wine glass and realizes she must have finished it while she was daydreaming so instead, she says "Yes please I'd love one a strawberry daiquiri please." as the man walks away Elisa is proud and happy that she had the nerve to order something a little more exotic.

The man returns and sits beside Elisa. She notices that he is wearing an Armani suit and a gold Rolex watch loaded with diamonds. Elisa is impressed as the little girl in her takes over. Elisa listens intently as the man talks about his life and she giggles at the right moments. Elisa becomes flushed as the man grabs her right hand and has his leg slide over to hers and their thighs touch.

As they finish their drinks the man gently grabs a firm grip on Elisa's hand and escorts her to the now packed dance floor. The music is fast for the first few songs and Elisa is having a great time. In the fifth song, the man gently pulls Elisa to him and firmly grips her waist as they sway to a slow song. Elisa feels her head spinning as her attraction to her good-looking partner grows. At the end of the third consecutive slow song the music picks up the pace and the man leads Elisa back to their seats. At the bar, Elisa smiles and says "Will you please excuse me I have to go powder my nose."

As Elisa walks to the washroom her head spinning from the excitement, she can't believe she has never come to the club before this. Her mind has completely forgotten about her work. While she is in the washroom Elisa misses her man ordering more drinks and also him pouring a vile full of clear liquid into her daiquiri.

Elisa returns to her seat with a wide smile on her face as the man hands her, her drink and says "to new friends and I hope a whole lot more." Elisa practically gulps her drink down hesitating only slightly due to the cold ice hurting on the way down. As they finish the drinks the man again escorts a willing Elisa back out onto the dance floor. As the music floods her senses Elisa bounces to the beat enthusiastically.

Elisa stumbles as her head starts to spin but her man grabs hold of her to let her regain her balance then says" My darling let's go outside and get some fresh air. I think the daiquiris has gotten to you." Elisa is lead outside where the air starts her head spinning even more. The two staggers down the street and around the corner into an alley where a white B M W pulls up and the man opens the back door and slides Elisa inside. He climbs in afterward on top of her to stop her from struggling. It didn't matter because the drug has now knocked Elisa into a deep unconscious state.

A groggy Elisa wakes up to discover she is lying on an uncomfortable table, on her back naked. Her arms and legs are bound to the table's legs and a rubber ball has been shoved in her mouth and duct tape fastened across her mouth making calling for help impossible. Elisa pulls at her restraints as panic sets in but that just causes the metal cuffs to dig painfully into her wrists and ankles. She gives up trying as two men enter the room, one is her dance partner the other is an older burly balding man. It is clear why the Italian-looking man was chosen to try and entice Elisa into their clutches. The burly man walks over to Elisa as her dance partner starts to talk" Elisa Levi, we know you are an Israeli spy, so we are going to gather some information from you. Don't be mistaken we are going to get any information you know; you will be severely tortured and then killed. It's just a matter of how painful and long this will be. The sooner you talk the sooner it will be over." As the good-looking man talked the ugly man fondled Elisa's body roughly, then he ripped the tape from Elisa's mouth. He inserts his hand to remove the rubber ball and Elisa takes a bite out of his finger. The man cries out in pain as his index finger snaps. He is finally able to remove his hand and viciously slaps Elisa's face. He walks out of the room for a minute and returns with a red-hot poker that he sadistically shows to Elisa saying" Okay you chose the more painful route; this pleases me so now I'm in charge. My partner had grown fond of you the last few days and started to want to take it easier on you but no luck now I'm in charge." as the burly man stops talking his voice is replaced by Elisa's screams as the red-hot poker burns deeply into each thigh. When she stops screaming Elisa notices a sickening aroma in the air, then realizes it's the smell of her burning flesh.

The man continues to come back asking Elisa questions four or five times a day. Each time Elisa musters the strength not to talk partly out of hatred to the man and also under the belief that the longer she holds out although immensely painful and humiliating, she believes her fellow agents will rescue her. Each time the man uses cigarettes on her and a thick belt with a heavy metal buckle.

On the fifth day of the beatings and the men helping themselves to her body, Elisa finally breaks and starts talking. Her body is covered from head to toe in lacerations and bruises as well as burns. The beatings and rapes continue for another three days even though there is nothing more that Elisa can tell until she is finally set free by a knife slitting her esophagus causing her to slowly suffocate.

Back in Israel, the Massaud calls the United States state department giving them a copy of the message Elisa had intercepted. The FBI goes on high alert looking for possible terrorists.

CHAPTER THREE

SOMEWHERE ON THE AFGHAN PAKISTAN BORDER OCTOBER SAME YEAR

Alex Trovski the contact for the Russian mob enters a small farmhouse where he is to meet three Al Qaeda terrorists. Alex is a forty-four-year-old experienced ex-KGB operative, he stands 5'8" tall and is a muscular 165 pounds, his face is weathered and his hair starting to grey. The three Al Qaeda members enter with scarves covering their faces. Alex shakes their hands and asks "How does the poppy crop this year?" Majid the tallest of the Al Qaeda members is also the leader he replies "It's a great crop this year. Since our warlords have been negotiating with the Americans, the Americans have stopped napalming our fields. This has allowed us to produce two and a half times the crop as last year." Majid removes his scarf now that he realizes that Alex is the man they are supposed to meet. Majid stands at five foot ten and has a short body with unusually long legs. His face and hands are weathered and callused from the thirty hard years he has spent in the rugged mountains of Afghanistan. Alex asks "Have the Americans started to use the opium like you had our troops use it in the eighties? That was a brilliant strategy."

"No, not yet they seem too disciplined for that. I guess after Viet Nam and what happened to your troops, they have become more aware of the dangers of smoking opium in a combat area." Answers Majid.

"Well, that's good news for us about the poppy fields because demand is higher than ever," says Alex Trovski.

"So why the rush meeting?" inquires Majid.

"Because I have a proposal to pass on to you from my superiors." says Alex "We have learned that on the last weekend of March in Chicago there will be a meeting between the crime bosses from New York, Chicago and Miami. They will be meeting at the National kitchen and bath show."

"So how does this affect us?" asks Majid.

"Patience and let me finish. You have been looking for an opportunity to strike inside the United States again. So now I am offering you one. First, you get six operatives into the States and we will arrange the time and location for the attacks." explains Alex then after taking a deep breath Alex continues "Two men with a bomb each made up of plastic explosives and ball bearings will enter the convention center. The first will walk up to the targets we supply and detonate his bomb. The second will head for the main exit and set off his bomb when the lobby is full from the rush of people running out after the first blast. This should give you a very high kill rate and the second-largest terror attack within the United States, showing the arrogant Americans that they still aren't safe. But that's not all the other four operatives will be at a restaurant in Chicago where three members of the Japanese Yakuza are scheduled to meet one of our Armenian operatives. Your four men will be armed with automatic weapons and have bombs strapped to their bodies. The Japanese men must be killed first. You will also be glad to know that this restaurant's client consists mainly of affluent Jewish families as long as your men are successful in killing our targets, we will have plenty of jobs for you down the line. The beauty of these attacks is it gives you a huge victory over the States while at the same time the terror attacks cover up our motives for killing our targets."

After he is finished talking Alex opens his briefcase and hands Majid, thirty thousand American dollars and says "This should cover most of your expenses for the jobs."

Majid takes the cash and says "I already have the six men in mind two are oriental and the other four are Arabic. All are very dedicated to our cause."

"Get your men into the States and I will have our coordinator contact them to give them directions and some more money," adds Alex

Alex then heads back across the border to Iran. Where he flies from Tehran to Rome and then off to Toronto where the head of the North American division the Russian mob resides and operates.

CHAPTER FOUR

CHICAGO
ONE YEAR EARLIER

Dave Gellar sits in his office going over notes on possible terror groups in the Chicago area while he feels pangs of guilt for leaving his wife Susan alone at home so much with their two boys Ryan and Stuart. Ryan is twelve and suffers from autism causing his interaction with others to be retarded. Stuart is fourteen and is very much into sports. Dave stands at six foot three and two hundred and thirty-five pounds. Dave is muscular and fit, with short dark hair and brown eyes. Dave and Susan have been married for twenty years.

Dave's daydreaming is suddenly interrupted by the ringing of his phone.

"Dave its Raphael Torres, I think I have some important information for you. Can we meet right away at the usual location?" Dave ponders with guilt about working late again and missing dinner with his family again then replies" Okay Raphael it is an hour to the bar, so I'll be there around seven o'clock."

Dave hangs up and immediately phones Susan and explains that he won't be getting home until after eight-thirty. Dave gets up and heads into Bill Johnson's office. Bill Johnson is Dave's boss. Bill is a surly man, 53 years old standing five foot nine inches, and a plump two hundred thirty pounds. Bill feels he should be further up in the FBI because his dad was district manager. Bill is jealous of Dave because Dave gets calls from Washington all the time. Dave informs his boss about the discussions, but Bill still feels slighted.

"What is it, Dave?" asks bill with irritation in his voice.

"I just got a call from one of my informants Raphael Torres, He wants to meet. So, I'm heading to our location at seven o'clock. I will inform you in the morning on what he has to say," explains Dave.

"Isn't he that drug dealer?" asks Bill with a shrug like it is a hopeless cause going.

"Well, he was a drug smuggler and a very good one. He gave a lot of information when we arrested him and now, he has been out of jail for four years without any trouble," explains Dave.

"Whatever," replies Bill showing his lack of interest.

Dave leaves the office and heads off to meet Raphael frustrated at Bill Johnson's obvious snub. The traffic is heavy so Dave arrives at the bar at seven-thirty. Raphael is sitting off in a corner booth nursing a beer. Dave goes to the bar and grabs two more. Dave walks over and sits across from Raphael. Raphael is a forty-year-old man with dark hair and a dark complexion. He is five foot eight inches tall and a slight one hundred and sixty-five pounds. Raphael has an eight-inch scar running down his right cheek courtesy of his prior life as a drug runner. He has told Dave since he got out of prison that he looks at the scare as an incentive to stay away from the dangers of the drug trade.

Dave takes a sip of his beer then slides an envelope across the table to Raphael. Raphael opens the envelope and takes out three hundred dollars. "What's this for?" asks Raphael.

"You said you had some information, and this is our usual agreement of payment," responds Dave.

"Thanks, Dave but this is big I just thought you should know. I was contacted last month to smuggle in a planeload of wine from Germany. I almost agreed then a little alarm went off in my head, so I looked into it deeper. My first thought was that it was going to be a drug shipment, then I really got suspicious when my contact turned out to be Adolph Bremer of the Arian Nation. Dave, I called your office and got that Bill Johnson guy, but I left a message for you." explains Raphael.

"I never got the message Raphael." responds a growingly irritated Dave.

"Well, I made the decision to follow up and do the job. I still thought it was drugs but figured I could get back to you as soon as I arrived back. Also, the whole plan is on my computer and my wife is going to forward it to you if something went wrong. So, I went to Germany and met Hans Schmidt, a local neo-Nazi member. I still think it was just drugged suggested that they enclose the drugs in sealed rubber containers and insert them when full into a green-tinted wine bottle then fill the bottle up and cork and seal it. I then made arrangements for a member of this group in Chicago who owned a wine shop to order the crates of wine. So once the paperwork was done to make it look like an official order the crates were loaded on a plane and I was to escort the shipment into O'Hare airport. I arrived with the wine last Tuesday. When the customs was there checking the paperwork I deliberately dropped a crate that I knew was just wine, breaking the bottles The agents then knew the shipment was wine and never suspected that we would be smuggling drugs inside the expensive wine bottle." Raphael now nervous downs the beer that Dave brought him then takes a breath to compose himself and continues "That's when things got really interesting Dave. The pilot was also a member of the Arian Nation and he looked scared. Then he told me as we escorted the wine via truck to the shop, that he was startled by my prank because he didn't know that I had this clumsy escort routine planned out. It was then that I guess his nerves took over and he told me their secret. It was not drugs inside those containers but fifty pounds of powdered anthrax."

Dave was aghast by the story, with his mind racing to all the possibilities that a group like the Arian Nation could do with that much anthrax. "Raphael this is great information thank you. After we locate this shipment, you will receive a huge reward from the government" says Dave.

"That would be nice Dave, but I really have wanted to find something to give you as information since you turned my life around and helped me get that plea bargain otherwise, I would have been in jail until my son graduated from college." responds Raphael as he slides a piece of paper across the table to Dave explaining "This is a list of all the Chicago members that I met and their locations, Dave, I hope it helps you."

"Raphael this is all too great! We will get on this right away and can I suggest you take your wife and son and go on a vacation for a month or so. Just in case the skinheads are smart enough to link you to us getting the information." suggests Dave.

Dave leaves the bar and tries to phone Bill Johnson to inform him that they have a hot lead, but Bill has his cell phone turned off. So, an equally excited and frustrated Dave drives his hour-long trip back to his house and Susan. Just realizing then that he had talked for so long to Raphael that it was already nine-thirty.

Dave calls his wife to explain that he won't get home until after ten-thirty. Susan sounds disappointed but says "It's all right Dave. As long as the meeting went well, and I will heat up some of the casseroles for you so it's hot when you get home. You must be so hungry."

"Yeah, honey I am thanks," replies Dave.

"Dave I also got your old packman game set up downstairs for the kids. There is a packman tournament coming to town in two weeks and you would be so shocked, Ryan is a natural he beats Stuart every time," says Susan excitedly because Ryan is autistic, and she is just happy to see him enjoying himself.

The next morning Dave arrives at the office early and rushes into Bill Johnson's office to tell him all he learned from his meeting with Raphael Torres. Bill is on the phone talking to his sister then he looks up and says "Dave don't you knock? I'm busy here come back at nine" Dave takes a deep sigh and bolts out of the office to grab a coffee that he takes into his office for his hours wait.

At nine sharp Dave returns to Bill Johnson's office where Dave exaggerates his knock-on Bill's door. An annoyed Bill nods for Dave to come in and take a seat. Dave pulls up a chair and straddles it facing Bill and begins "I have some solid information that fifty pounds of anthrax are in the hands of a local Arian Nation group in Chicago."

"Our definition of solid must be different Dave, the way I see it you have the word of a drug smuggler who has been inactive for six years. He is probably just looking for a little money and maybe some attention. Why on earth would a white Supremes group like Arian

Nation hire a Hispanic like Raphael for such an important role?" questions a sarcastic Bill.

"Maybe because he is known as the best smuggler over the last twenty years. And Raphael gave us the information we used to arrest and convict fourteen drug dealers six years ago. It was one of our largest and most successful drug operations. Also, I know this man personally and I think I can trust him and his information much more than some of my superiors." blasts Dave regretting he took such an aggressive and insulting stand.

"Well smart ass if you think I'm going to spend valuable dollars and manpower on your little goose chase. You're crazy. I don't have time for this shit Gellar get out and get some real work done." screams Bill intentionally loud enough so that the whole office could hear him dressing down Dave.

A red-faced and angry Dave heads back to his office and slams his door.

After sitting in his office for a couple of hours steaming Dave notices that most of the office has gone to lunch when he hears a light knock at the door. Dave looks up and sees Rasheed Sing standing waiting to be invited in. Rasheed is a twenty-two-year-old computer expert. Rasheed stands a slight five foot ten one hundred and forty-five pounds, his family came to Chicago from India when Rasheed was eighteen. Rasheed works in the research department at the office. "Hi Rasheed can I help you?" asks Dave

"Actually Mr. Gellar I was hoping I could help you. I couldn't help but overhear your conversation with Mr. Johnson and I was thinking that I could do the research for you," explains Rasheed.

"Rasheed I would appreciate it but Johnson would crucify you if he caught you helping me." cautions Dave.

"Well, he never stays past six o'clock so I can work on it after hours," says Rasheed trying to convince Dave to let him help.

"Okay, Rasheed I really could use the help. Here is a list of the people and locations I have been given, please see what you can find out." finishes Dave relieved that he has help

Dave and Rasheed work checking for the members of this particular group and their addresses until nine o'clock then Dave calls it a night and heads home.

Dave walks through the door to his house at ten to ten and Stuart is waiting for him dressed in his Pop Warner football uniform. "Look dad I got number twelve, Jim Kelly's old number, and my team is called the Bills. I made quarterback and safety on the team and I even won the job as the punter," exclaims Stuart excitedly

"That's great son when is your first game?" asks Dave.

"Saturday morning dad at ten, can you come? Asks Stuart

"I don't know Stuart I'll have to see about my work," replies Dave

Susan comes down the stairs from putting Ryan to bed. Susan stands at five foot six weighing a hundred and thirty pounds. Susan has dark brown shoulder-length wavy hair and big brown eyes. Dave and Susan met as sophomores at Northwestern University and got married three years later. They just celebrated their twentieth anniversary two weeks ago. Susan looks at her husband and says "You better go say goodnight to your son he scored the highest score on the packman machine today beating your old record from your university days. I also have dinner in the oven. Pork chops in mushroom gravy and scalloped potatoes. Your sister called today she's coming down from Milwaukee tomorrow to stay for a couple of weeks. Maybe we can set her up with James or Tony while she's here."

"I don't know about that Suzy April is still pretty pissed off at men since she caught her fiancée cheating on her," responds Dave as he hugs his wife then heads upstairs to say good night to Ryan. Dave follows Susan into the kitchen where he gets his dinner and a Pepsi and sits down to eat not realizing until know that he hasn't eaten all day. Susan grabs a tea and sits down with Dave as he eats.

"You would be amazed at the way Ryan has picked up that video game. If I recall you were the dorm champion at packman and after a couple of days, he is already beating your old scores. It's almost like he goes into a trance. He laughs every time the ghosts change, and he can eat them. And Stuart's football coach says he is the best rookie in the league. They start this Saturday. They play eight games then the playoffs." says Susan filling Dave in on what the family has been up to.

"Did April say why she is coming?" asks Dave.

"Dave she is your sister, and she was so young when your dad died that you are like her father. Remember you are seventeen years older than her and with your mom living in phoenix now we are the only family she has. Besides I love April, we have fun together and it's going to be nice talking to an adult for a change," says Susan

With Stuart already putting himself to bed Dave cleans up the kitchen and then he and Susan decide to take advantage of the quiet house and go to bed early for a change.

Dave gets up early so that he can get into work before anyone else especially Bill Johnson. Dave shows up at the FBI office at a quarter to six and is shocked to see Rasheed has beaten him in and is printing some pages at the computer.

"Good Morning Rasheed I'm going downstairs for coffee, how do you take yours?" asks Dave.

"Thank you Mr. Gellar I take mine double, double, please. I'm running off the names and addresses of all forty-nine known members of this local chapter of the Arian Nation. It should be ready for you to see when you get back upstairs." reports Rasheed

Dave returns with two large coffees and two large cinnamon buns. Rasheed hands Dave ten pages of printed-out information on the Arian Nation chapter and Dave starts to look over the work Rasheed has done while they both enjoy their early morning caffeine and sugar rush. This list includes all forty-nine members' names and home addresses as well as their jobs and even their ranks in the group. But most impressive to Dave is that on Adolph Bremer the leader Rasheed has found Adolph's parents' address and even his girlfriend's address. AS Dave finishes his bun, he says "Rasheed this is great work thank you."

"I'm far from done Mr. Gellar there's still a lot of research on this group. I tracked down the e-mails of each member from the Arian nation website. These people think that we can't trace them back to their computer and server through their e-mail address. I also researched Ingrid Lowe, Adolph's girlfriend and found out that she recently purchased a rundown home on Cherry Lane, even though there is no record of her working anywhere over the last two years. Her bank account has never had more than five hundred dollars in it until two months ago when she received a twenty-five-thousand-dollar check from the national chapter of the Arian Nation. She has also deposited five deposits of five thousand dollars in cash over the last two months. There was also an attack on twenty squatters at the Cherry Lane address one week before Ingrid bought the house for surprise, surprise forty-five thousand dollars with no mortgage.

The squatters that were beat up have since moved to another part of town stating that the attackers told them that if they ever came back, they would be beaten to death. No arrests were ever made but the witnesses said that all the attackers wore black gloves and hoods. They also were all identified as white and using racial slurs." reports Rasheed

"Rasheed you are amazing that was all retrieved in just one day's work. Did you even go home last night?" asks Dave.

"No sir I got started and was having so much fun. I grabbed an hour's sleep on the table around three o'clock." explains Rasheed.

"Okay Rasheed it's a quarter after eight we better get to our regular stations Bill will be here soon.' suggests Dave.

Dave goes to his office and pulls out the tedious work on private airport security checks that Bill Johnson had given him to do. Background checks are usually done by the research department not by field agents but after Dave's successful arrests of a sleeper cell in Gary Indiana Dave has noticed that Bill has tried to keep him out of the field. Dave's suspects that Bill is still threatened by Dave's close connections in Washington.

As soon as Bill Johnson arrived at the office, he calls Dave in to see him. Dave thinking that Bill has discovered Rasheed and his work gathers the anger to finally tell Bill that he is going to go over Bill's head on this case, but when he gets to bill's office, he is surprised to see Bill has brought a coffee in for him, so Dave sits down with the coffee ready to listen to what Bill has to say.

"Dave I was thinking last night, you should get Raphael what's his name picked up and brought in for questioning. I think if something is going on he is part of it, and under the patriot act we can hold him for a few days without anyone knowing and get some proper interrogation started on him," suggests Bill trying to take control of the case and usurp Dave's influence.

A now furious Dave makes it his turn to turn on Bill Johnson, but Dave is too disciplined to yell so that the rest of the office can hear like Bill did the day before. So, he starts "In all respect detective Johnson, have you totally lost touch with reality? First, if we were to pick up Raphael and bring him in and he was in on the plan that would just alert the others to change some of their plans and become more careful. Second, Raphael is not involved and is trying to help us out by reporting what he knows. He was here he is a proud man, and we would only lose one of our most trustworthy informants. Third I have worked on my own after hours and gathered some pretty good leads and fourth I told Raphael to get his family and head out on a vacation for a month or so and he did."

A steamed Bill responds saying in a screaming voice once again so that the whole office can hear him" Gellar you've gone too far this time you are not welcome in this office for another week." Then in a quieter voice so that nobody can hear the rest Bill adds" You have a lot of friends at high places and a good record so I can't suspend you without drawing too much attention to this office. You stay away from here until next Thursday and then you and I are going to work on your transfer request to another local."

"You can keep me out of the office but I am going to continue working on this case and keep up on my reports so that there is a complete record and as far as the transfer no friggin way when I do get back, I'm going straight back to my job and I better be back in the field or I will call one of my contacts that you fear so much." finishes Dave as he gets up and leaves behind a shocked Bill Johnson.

As soon as Dave gets in his car, he hears his cell phone number is from the office. After debating whether to answer the phone or not thinking that it is Bill Johnson, Dave decides to answer and is pleasantly surprised to hear Rasheed Sing's voice "Dave I went to the accounting office to use the phone, but I just wanted you to know you can get me on my private cell phone anytime and I will call you on yours. I am going to continue to work late and come in early to see what I can find out."

"Hey Rasheed, be careful you're new and Johnson will cut you a new asshole if he catches you helping me on this. I on the other hand have almost twenty years' experience here and probably have many more friends in the FBI than Bill does. How about meeting me at Ditka's steakhouse tonight at nine and my expense account will buy us dinner." asks Dave.

"That would be nice Mr. Gellar but you know I'm Hindu so no meat for me," explains Rasheed.

"Rasheed that's not a problem but it explains why you're so thin." Dave tries to joke then continues "Ditka's has a huge salad bar, and they have pasts and vegetables so please come and have dinner I need a friend on the force." says Dave. Rasheed is pleased that Dave called him a friend so he happily accepts and says" I will work until a quarter to nine then meet you in the bar Mr. Gellar thank you."

"One thing Rasheed you're my friend you have to start calling me Dave, and it is I that should be thanking you. So far you have supplied all the leads." encourages Dave

"Okay then Dave sees you at nine," confirms Rasheed beaming with pride.

On his way home Dave decides to go check out the house on Cherry Lane and is not surprised to see that black curtains have been set up in every window so that nobody can see inside. The house is a small bungalow probably built just after world war two when there was a housing boom on the southwest side of Chicago for all the returning war veterans. Dave also notices that this run-down property has now got flowers planted and the lawn cut. So, he figures that there is someone living their full time so he decides to stake out the house from down the street to see who enters and leaves.

Dave is able to snap pictures of four men and a woman that he sees entering and leaving the house before he remembers that his sister has driven down from Milwaukee to visit. The time is now six-thirty already so Dave immediately heads home.

CHAPTER FIVE

Dave arrives home and hears a noise coming from the basement, so he heads straight downstairs where he sees Stuart laughing at April. Stuart says" See Aunt April, I told you, you would never bear Ryan he's won five in a row." April gives Ryan a hug, but Ryan is only interested in getting back to the packman game. Dave is so pleased Ryan has never shown this much interest in anything before.

April sees her brother and rushes over to give him a hug saying" Nice of you to finally show. Your wife has gone to get Kentucky fried chicken and salads for dinner. Dave your sons are little hustlers; Stuart makes the bets and Ryan kicks my ass." April is an extremely pretty woman five foot three inches tall and weighing only one hundred and three pounds her hair is blond and falls about four inches below her shoulders. Her eyes are deep green like emeralds she has petite measurements thirty-two b chest her waist is twenty-two and her hips thirty-two. April has always attracted men but at twenty-eight she has yet to find one that has treated her well. She thought she had one once two years ago and got engaged but at Christmas, he gave her a present when she opened it she saw a diamond engagement ring with a one karat diamond which was larger than the one she already was wearing. April immediately knew something was wrong then she looked at her fiancée who had gone pure white. The next day April discovered that he had been seeing his ex-girlfriend for the last four months when his ex-called her to talk. During the conversation, April found out that the other woman had received a pair of emerald earrings with a note saying to my love April I got these because they remind me of your eyes, and they are your birthstone. The ex and April talked for an hour when April found out the ex-dumped April's fiancée too, the woman laughed about the situation, but April had been deeply hurt and has refused every offer for a date since.

Susan arrives with the chicken just as Dave, April, and the boys run up the stairs.

"I'll go put the chicken in the oven to keep warm Dave you go get the kids washed up while April and I grab a glass of wine," says Susan as she rushes to the kitchen and puts the salads in the fridge and the chicken in the oven at one hundred and fifty degrees to keep it warm. Susan tells April to sit down and drink her wine while she sets the dining room table with six plates and sets of cutleries and four wine glasses. April notices the table and asks, "Okay Suzy why the four wine glasses Stuart and Ryan aren't old enough and six plates?"

"I met a friend at the store he's a really nice guy April a lawyer and I invited him over for dinner," explains Susan.

"Susan you better not be trying to set me up," responds April.

"He's just a nice guy April, it won't hurt you to talk." suggests Susan.

Susan and April finish their second glass of wine just as James Hunter arrives. James this is Dave's little sister April, and April this is James." April shakes James's hand. James is a balding forty-year-old man standing five foot eight inches tall and sporting a portly two hundred and thirty-five pounds. Not the type of guy that April usually falls for. The six sat down for dinner and James is almost overly polite the whole time thanking Susan repeatedly for inviting him over and April's only awkward moment came when he went out of his way to mention that he is divorced with no children. Dave sensing April's discomfort changes the subject" James Stuart her is his football team's starting quarterback and safety for this season. His coach says he is the youngest quarterback in the league. Stuart Mr. Hunter was the starting center at Indiana University for three years."

"Wow Mr. Hunter you must have been really good," exclaims Stuart

"Well Stuart football was a lot of fun and without getting a scholarship to go to university I never would have been able to become a lawyer," answers James in a friendly matter talking to Stuart as though he were an adult. April is impressed by James's good nature, but she is still not ready to date but has to admit the night wasn't a total disaster.

After the boys are put to bed James says "I better get going I have a court case starting at nine tomorrow. Thanks again for dinner Susan and April it was very nice meeting you. Good luck with your teaching career and your first season next year as coach of the schools' girls' varsity basketball team." April is relieved that James didn't try to ask her out because she would have hated to say no because he was such a nice man, but she also had absolutely no interest in going on a date with him.

James leaves and Susan David and April sit in the living room to talk. April takes a sip of her coffee and says "Now that was kind of awkward Susan, thanks."

"Oh, don't worry April Tony is much better looking," adds Dave to his dismayed sister. Susan tries to avoid April's scolding look then she adds "Yeah April but Tony is a successful stockbroker and he is also a model in beer and car commercials, looks it's just dinner on Saturday then maybe a drink or two after. Besides April when you're here, it's the only time that I can drag Dave away from the office to go out."

"Okay Susan I'll go. Tonight, wasn't so terrible but promise me, if I want to go, we go. Also, promise that this is your last attempt at matchmaker for the rest of the trip." pleads April.

"Okay April but this guy is rich, successful, and extremely gorgeous," says Susan happy that April is at least pretending to be interested in dating again.

Dave explains that he won't be in the office for a week, but instead of telling Susan about his blow-up with Bill Johnson, he instead says he will be working surveillance in the field for a while. The three adults finish their coffees and head off to bed for the night.

The next morning Dave decides to check out the house on Cherry Lane again. This time it is bustling with people carrying boxes. Dave is able to get pictures of an additional twenty-two men and three more women so He phones Rasheed on his cell phone. Rasheed answers and says "Dave I'm really sorry about last night I tried to get you on your cell phone to tell you I couldn't make our dinner, but it must have been turned off." Dave feels horrible because he forgot all about the dinner with his little sister in town, but feeling relieved he tells Rasheed "Don't worry about it Rasheed, we can make it tonight, and in the meantime can you meet me at lunch at the crispy cream on Butler avenue? I've got some pictures that I was hoping you could print and maybe get some information on the people for me." Request Dave.

"Yes, on all three counts Dave, I can meet you for lunch, grab the discs and download the pictures. I can then check them against any photo identification. I should have all the names and addresses of the people by working on it after the office clears. I can then give you all the information that I gather at dinner tonight. Say we try nine o'clock again at Ditka's again? I promise I will be there this time Mr. Gellar. I mean Dave." says Rasheed.

"Great Rasheed I don't know what I'd do on this case without your help." confirms a greatly relieved and embarrassed Dave.

Dave shows up at the Crispy cream early and grabs a coffee while he waits for Rasheed to arrive. Rasheed shows up looking exhausted at ten after twelve.

"Rasheed you better get some sleep tonight. It looks like you slept in your clothes. I learned to always take a second outfit in my car just in case." suggests Dave.

Dave hands the discs over to Rasheed and Rasheed hurries off to get back to the office figuring he can download the pictures while everybody is at lunch, then he can get started referencing the government-issued identifications of all the names he has then cross-reference them with the pictures Dave gave him. Rasheed says bye and rushes off leaving Dave alone to drink his second coffee.

At three o'clock Dave decides he will go take some time to watch Stuart at his football practice, then go home to see April and Susan before heading out for dinner with Rasheed.

Dave quickly spots Stuart as his Bills team is scrimmaging against the Packers. Dave has arrived just in time to see his fourteen-year-old son throws a perfect thirty-yard pass into the hands of a receiver streaking down the middle of the seam. Dave gets a lump of pride in his throat that only grows as Stuart completes eight out of ten passes and then when the team starts running the option series Stuart controls the ball perfectly. While he is watching the Bills score three touchdowns to none by the Packers. Stuart throws two touchdown passes.

Dave is lost in pride watching his son when out of nowhere he gets hit from behind. Surprised by the sudden attack Dave loses his balance and falls. His training almost kicks in but luckily it doesn't too soon as he looks up into the laughing face of April. April has arrived to drive Stuart home from practice. "Dave it's great that you came Stuart has been dying for you to see him play," says April.

"Well, he sure is a good player and most of the players are a year older than him." beams Dave.

"Well, why don't you drive him home and tell him how good he was? He'd like that. So, I'll just let him know I was here then I'll run to the wine store and grab a bottle of merlot for Suzy and I. At least there are no surprise setups today, thank God." Dave laughs at his sister then waits for Stuart to finish listening to his coach. April isn't so patient so she playfully walks over to the huddle and playfully grabs Stuart by the face mask and says his father will drive him home while she runs a couple of errands. Stuart is excited his father has come to watch him, so he turns and scans the sidelines and waves to his dad.

All the way home Dave tells his son how proud he is of him, and that he is really not only looking good physically but he's even more impressed by Stuart's knowledge of the offense and his positioning on defense.

They drop in at the Dairy Queen on the way home and Dave buys three large chocolate shakes for his two sons and himself, figuring that the women will be drinking the wine instead.

When Dave and Stuart arrive home Dave's instincts prove to be wrong as April and Susan's eyes pop out looking at the milkshakes. But after teasing Dave for not buying them a shake April says jokingly" It's really a good thing Dave because I don't want to get fat." After Dave and Susan laugh for a minute over April worrying about gaining weight on her one hundred- and three-pound petite figure. Dave heads upstairs and has a shower.

Dave says goodbye to his family at eight-thirty and heads out to have dinner with Rasheed still thankful that Rasheed also didn't show up the night before but feeling guilty for letting Rasheed believe that it was his fault. Dave is also disappointed that he has to leave his family because everything is going so well. His older son looks like a star in Dave's favorite sport and he has never seen Ryan as happy or comfortable as he seems now.

When Dave shows up at Ditka's, he spots Rasheed sitting waiting in the bar sipping on a large Pepsi. Dave walks over and says, "Rasheed you're not at work you are allowed something stronger than that."

"I don't drink alcohol Dave, but I have some good news maybe about your pictures. I have identified all the men and women except two men, from their driver's licenses or their age of majority cards. They are all members of that Arian Nation list we have. The even better news is that an agent in the organized crime unit named Harley Simpson is getting a search warrant for the property based on the possibility of drug sales due to the property being purchased in cash. He will also call you for tomorrow's raid. He and three of his agents yourself and Darius Gentry from your department will take part in the raid. Should be sometime around two in the afternoon said, Harley. Dave, you have a lot of friends from all departments in this force. Bill Johnson knows nothing of the raid," explains Rasheed.

"That's unbelievably good news Rasheed." exclaims a happy Dave.

The two men get up after Rasheed finishes his Pepsi and Dave finishes his beer and head to the restaurant section for their dinners. Rasheed orders a salad bar and pasta Prima Vera; Dave gets the Caesar salad and coconut shrimp as appetizers the for the main course Dave orders the twenty once baseball steak and baked potatoes. Both men enjoy their meal and the bonding.

Both men leave the restaurant excited about what they may find the next day and Dave is also happy about having a new ally on the force as well as still beaming over his home life being so good.

Rasheed is just thrilled that after working two years he is finally feeling like he is a major contributor to the solving of a case.

Dave arrives back home at eleven thirty and finds that the women also seem to be enjoying themselves giggling and talking. Dave notices that the bottle of merlot is empty being partially responsible for the women's good moods.

CHAPTER SIX

The next morning Dave heads to his stake out position at the house on Cherry Lane to keep an eye on the house until the other agents show up with the warrant. This time Dave quietly puts on a flak jacket so that Susan doesn't see him wearing it.

The house is surprisingly quiet as only one man and two women have been spotted entering the house by Dave as noon approaches. Dave eats his lunch in the car while watching the house, a subway Italian sub, and a Pepsi.

At one-thirty Dave's phone rings and it's his partner Darius Gentry. Darius tells Dave that they have the warrant and the four of them will be there just before two.

Dave spots the black Ford Bronco pull up and park across the street from the house, so Dave climbs out of his car and holsters his gun. Dave then walks up and meets the other five agents. Darius introduces Dave to Harley and the other three agents. Harley and one of the other agents head to the back of the house to seal off that escape route. Dave is happy to discover that the door is still the original cheap wooden door and wasn't replaced by a metal door. The two agents from Harley's unit walk back to the Ford Bronco to get a battering ram to knock down the front door. Dave is now happy about the black curtains in every window. What at first was an annoyance preventing him from seeing inside the house has now become a tool preventing anybody inside from seeing them.

Dave calls Harley at the back of the house on his phone to give him the one-minute signal. The four men at the front get ready as Dave watches the time. At the minute time, Dave motions to the two agents to proceed. These are the two largest men both young and strong. They pull the battering ram back and smash the door in on their first thrust. In the back Harley and his partner take cover and aim their guns at the back door.

In the front, the four men burst into the house with Dave leading the way guns drawn. There were two shocked women sitting on the couch with swastikas tattooed on their upper left arms. Just as it appears that the raid has totally caught the racists by surprise shots rang out from the yard. Dave and his team duck behind walls eyes staining for ant movement. Outside Harley calls the Chicago police for backup. Harley had a friend on the local force that he talked about the raid so they were already prepared to go as four cruisers with two officers each immediately respond to the call from a coffee shop where they were waiting, only two blocks away.

Just as things seemed to be quieting down Darius gets hit with a shot in his chest. The bullet knocks Darius to the ground as the bullet turns out to be an armour-piercing bullet that effortlessly penetrates through Darius's flak jacket. Dave and the other two agents open fire on the area that the shot came from. The two women drop to their knees with their hands on their heads as though they have been through scenes like this before. One agent cuffs the women and leads them outside as the four police cars arrive at the house. The other agent and Dave grab Darius by the armpits and legs and carry him outside.

Once outside Dave looks at Darius and immediately knows it's bad when he sees blood bubbling with air foaming out of his mouth. An ambulance also shows up, so Dave and the agent pick up Darius and rush him over to the medics. Knowing that the situation is too dangerous for the medics to get to Darius.

Outback Harley and his partner are still under heavy fire from the house. Harley has already dropped two of the Arian Nation members on their initial escape attempt. But now Harley and his partner are pinned down under heavy fire from the back of the house.

A twenty-member swat team arrives at the house and pumps in tear gas grenades into the house then Dave rushes to the back of the house just ahead of half of the swat team as Dave and the ten swat team members open heavy fire into the house the occupants return the fire with armour-piercing weapons one of the rounds hits Harley's partner in the leg.

The grenade launcher arrives at the back of the house and six more grenades are launched into the house. One grenade for each window, three upstairs, and three downstairs in the upstairs window one of the occupants tries to throw a smoking grenade back outside but is hit by three shots as he tries, causing him to fall out the window. The heavy thick blinds are now taking their effect on the people inside as the blinds are preventing the gas from getting outside through the broken windows.

The shooting from inside is getting noticeably slower as a second swat team arrives. These agents are equipped with automatic weapons and the order is given and four more grenades are launched into the house and all the agents and swat members open fire through all the windows at the same time until the shell-shocked occupants throw out the upstairs window a white bed sheet. The assault is called off to allow the occupants to surrender. Twenty-two men and one woman exit the house. As the prisoners are being searched for weapons and cuffed two explosions rock the house from inside. Dave and two of the swat agents rush inside to see with gas masks on. There is a fire that started in the kitchen. Downstairs Dave sees another fire has started also. Dave hollers to everyone to leave the masks on no matter what. Fearing that anthrax may be in the air. Dave still looking around spots in the laundry room that there are eight crates of wine and beside the laundry to lie fifty empty bottle that have had their necks cut off carefully. There are also pictures of Illinois Senator Akeem Ismail posted all over the basement with racist slogans and die soon written on them.

Dave grabs a couple of the bottles that are lying on the floor with the necks cut off as evidence then grabs as many papers as he can find and orders everyone outside the house until the fire is put out and the house is cleared by chemical test to make sure there is no anthrax floating around.

Once outside Dave rushes over to the medics to find out about Darius's condition. The medic says "I'm sorry sir but the man with the chest wound had no vital signs and we couldn't revive him. He was taken to Mercy hospital because it is the closest, but I don't think that there was much hope. The other agent we turnikeed his leg to stop the bleeding but he will be alright. We also have six dead bodies from inside the house and two from the yard. Twelve others were taken to hospital under escort for either gunshot wounds or from the tear gas.

At five o'clock the house is cleared to enter with the fires exterminated and the air cleared of having any anthrax in it.

Dave and Harley enter the house until the forensic team from Harley's department shows up. When the team arrives Dave and Harley decide to go grab a beer together at a local family restaurant called Michael's place. Once inside the bar each man sighs as they drink their beers reflecting on the day's events. The men sit in silence until Harley blurts out." Your boss is an asshole of the first degree. No wonder you guys bumped heads. With only myself and three other agents from our department I went and asked your boss for some manpower showing him the search warrant, and he said he would not waste manpower or money on some wild goose chase. "Some fuckin goose chases that fire power alone warranted the raid. I'm just glad we had backup and medical on standby from our local police." adds Harley.

The men finish their second beers and decide it is best to head to their families for the night. As he leaves Harley adds, "We are going to take over the investigation from our end and while you were in the washroom, I called my boss, and he would like you to continue your investigation from our unit. And we have also grabbed that Indian kid out of research to help. It was Rasheed that got the ball rolling on this case. He and Darius went to my captain and asked for help. Seeing the Arian Nation was listed as a criminal organization last year we were only too happy to get involved. Your captain is going to have a lot of explaining to do on why he refused to help us."

A depressed Dave agrees that he will go to Harley's department in the morning to see what the forensic team has come up with. As Dave drives home, he can't get the image of Darius lying on the ground with blood bubbling out of his mouth.

$$+ \diamond\diamond\diamond\diamond\diamond +$$

CHAPTER SEVEN

$$+ \diamond\diamond\diamond\diamond\diamond +$$

Dave arrives home and removes his flak jacket in the garage before entering the house. Susan and April see Dave and laugh at his filthy face and clothes. "Rough day at the office honey?" Comments Susan. Dave shocks the woman by saying" we had a big shootout, one officer died, and another is in hospital with a bullet in his leg. We also killed eight of the bad guys and arrested fourteen others."

Dinner that night is very quiet except for Stuart who can't stop talking about how good his football team is. All they eat for dinner is a quick spaghetti with meat sauce main course and a Caesar salad for an appetizer. Dave forces down the food but sits in silence throughout the dinner and is not bothered by the women at all. April cleans the plates up as Dave and Susan put the boys to bed then sit in the living room silently watching the news. April joins them with a glass of wine for her and Susan and a cold beer for Dave. As April sits down the local news shows the house where the shootout occurred. The girls instinctively gasp at the destruction that the house has suffered. There are even pictures off the action taken from own the street as the tear gas enveloped the house. And the swat team can be seen scrambling for position.

After seeing the footage of the news April kisses her brother on the cheek and says good night. Dave and Susan also decide that it's time for bed. Dave doesn't sleep but just stares into the dark bedroom contemplating how everything went so wrong.

The next morning Dave heads to the FBI office at seven o'clock but he gets off on a different floor and heads to the organized crime division to see if the forensic team had discovered anything. Dave is surprised to see that Rasheed has already been transferred to the organized crime unit to help out. Harley comes over to Dave and says" Good morning Dave how'd you sleep last night? I had a six of beer before I could drift off to sleep."

"Well at least you fell asleep, I didn't catch a wink of sleep last night." replies Dave.

"We have an eight o'clock briefing this morning from the forensic tea, Dave, so why don't we grab your friend Rasheed and we will all go downstairs and grab a coffee? I could definitely use a strong one. That beer from last night is catching up to me." states Harley. Then adding "That Rasheed kid is ridiculous I was talking to the cleaner this morning when I got here and he said that Rasheed was here all night. Every time the forensic team would find something he would run to hide computer and work away for an hour or so." Says Harley to Dave with admiration showing for the young Indian researcher.

Dave Rasheed and Harley all head down to the coffee shop, each looking as though they could bleed to death from the red in their eyes. Rasheed orders his usual double, double and Dave and Harley stair in amazement as Rasheed pours in three more packages of sugar. Harley says with a smile" Son if you only want sugar and caffeine why not order a Pepsi?"

"People look at me strangely if I order pop at breakfast." Responds Rasheed.

"Oh Rasheed you call it pop you're like a true Midwesterner now in the east we call it soda." says Harley. Who then adds "Rasheed you are what twenty four twenty five? In my mind you are old enough to drink soda anytime of the day you want. Don't worry what other people think. Some use a lot of salt or pepper with their food. Have whatever suits you best." preaches Harley, who then goes to the counter and returns with two more coffees and a large Pepsi for Rasheed. Dave smiles to himself liking Harley's style.

At a quarter to nine the three men becoming friends get up and head on up to the forensic meeting. Harley falls behind Dave and Rasheed. Dave figures that Harley will just catch up to him at the elevator when he catches Harley's voice saying loudly "Johnson you putz thanks for your help yesterday. By the way Gellar was right but checking both your records nobody in my department is surprised. My captain and I are both thinking of contacting Washington just to let them know how helpful you were during this operation." Dave looks back and sees Bill Johnson's face turning bright red either from anger or from embarrassment because the whole coffee shop is watching Bill. Bill's frustration grows further when he sees Dave at the elevator. Bill yells out hoping to gather some pride back and says to Dave loudly, so that everyone in the coffee shop can hear his outburst "Gellar I told you to stay home for the week. Now be in my office at nine thirty and we'll discuss your insubordination that cost Darius his life."

Dave continues to show restraint but Harley's Irish temper flares up as he yells at Bill Johnson in his loudest voice "Johnson you are a complete waste of air you fucking moron. If your daddy hadn't been such a good agent you never would have gotten past writing parking tickets on a small town police force. You are a completely useless twit. Dave and I are in a meeting trying to do your job stopping terrorists so he won't be in your office answering any questions at all." As Harley catches up to Dave and Rasheed at the elevator. Harley can't help but look back at the steaming Bill Johnson and add disrespectfully "Hey Billy just stay out of our way and let real agents do their work." The men climb aboard the elevator and Dave is real satisfied that Harley had said all the things that Dave had wanted to say. As the elevator door closed Dave couldn't resist one more look at the red faced Bill Johnson.

When they get upstairs Dave, Harley and Rasheed head directly to the conference room where Kenneth Ralph is waiting to start briefing them. Ken starts "We were able to recover quite a bit of valuable information from the house on Cherry Lane. First of all there was the expected racial crap condemning every minority within the country. But that was mostly just propaganda. The real interesting items were a connection we found with a German neo Nazi organization in Cologne. This backs up the information that your informant gave you Dave. We also found a suitcase full of gas masks that they surprisingly didn't know about during the raid or they would have been wearing them when the tear gas was shot into the house. Seeing that Adolf Bremer was not at the house nor his girlfriend or the two men we have yet to identify, we figured that they had the gas masks for emptying the bottles of wine and probably to use during their attack as well as any handling that they do with the anthrax setting up their plan. Rasheed took it upon himself to contact the German authorities and present the pictures of the two missing unidentified men to see if they could identify them. Sure enough both of the men are known high ranking members of the German Arian Nation. They also have a background working in a chemical plant so both would have the knowledge of how to handle anthrax safely. "Ken takes a drink of his coffee and his face scrunches up in displeasure then he continues "Yuck cold coffee. Anyways, we also found an uncommon amount of literature on Senator Akeem Ismail. They seem to be quite disturbed that he is so successful and may be the leading candidate as the presidential nominee of the Democratic Party in four years. He is an ideal target seeing he is both a black and a Muslim. The group also have the layout of the Chicago Westin Hotel where the senator is holding a fund raiser on Monday night. We figure that this is the most likely target of the anthrax attack. An all-points bulletin has been issued for Adolf Bremer, his girlfriend Ingrid and the two Germen nationals but there has been no luck so far."

When Ken is finished his briefing Dave decides to grab a coffee and swallow his pride. So he heads back to the anti-terror unit to fill Bill Johnson in on the case. Dave is half worried about the attack and half gloating that he was right in listening to Raphael. When Dave enters the anti-terror office he is greeted by his colleagues who are in a sombre mood do to the death of Darius Gentry. Dave seeing the solemn looks on his fellow agents' faces immediately stops his proud feeling of being correct and joins the rest of the team in remorse. Janet Johnson comes up to Dave and says "Dave we are so sorry about yesterday, we all should have been there on the raid to give you support. We all know about your personal battle with Bill and everybody here to a man agrees with you. Bill has become far too cautious for this job. We all just wish you had called us to help. We all would have given our time off to help." as she finishes Dave looks into Janet's usually pretty blue eyes as sees that they are red now from her obvious crying as the tears have made her makeup run. Dave thanks Janet for her comments then figures he's delayed long enough and heads to Bill Johnson's office.

As Dave enters Bill's office, Bill looks up and Dave can see Bill's hands shaking. Dave thinks it's from being upset about Darius then figures it's probably more likely that he is worried what the official report from the organized crime unit is going to say about him.

A worried Bill Johnson gestures for Dave to take a seat, so Dave does and then brings Bill up to date on all that has happened and what they think is going to be the Arian Nations next move. Dave then finishes saying "So we could really use some extra manpower to cover the Westin hotel on Monday night." Bill thinks for a minute then responds saying "I wish I could Dave but most of my people are going to be covering other areas of Chicago that night protecting other dignitaries visiting."

Dave falsely believing that Bill actually wants to help says' Well Bill this is a real solid lead and it should be our first priority on Monday." Bill shows his true feelings by saying "I thought you had left this department and you were working the organized crime scene now. You're such a good agent Dave that I'm sure that you and your new buddies will keep senator Ismail safe. Besides I've already lost one agent this week. I don't think I can risk losing anymore, especially to something as dangerous as anthrax."

Dave composes himself then gets up and calmly walks out of Bill's office and heads back to the organized crime unit. On his way out Janet says "Well things must be getting better we didn't hear Bill screaming."

"Not really Janet he is going to be no help." Counters Dave.

"Well Dave remember there are at least a dozen or so of us that are available to help you if it's after hours, just call please."

Dave walks back into the organized crime unit and Harley asks "Did you get anywhere with that thick headed jerk?"

"No he is not going to offer any help but we should head to the Westin now and get the itinerary of Mondays speech to see if we can figure out where and when the most likely times are for the attack." Answers Dave.

Dave and Harley drive to the Westin hotel and show the hotel manager their FBI badges. The manager says the person that is with the senator setting up the plans for Monday is Jason Armstrong, but Jason has stepped out for a couple of hours and the manager tells Dave and Harley to have lunch in the coffee shop and he will inform Jason to go see them as soon as he returns. The manager the calls the coffee shop and tells them to supply the lunch to Dave and Harley on the hotels bill.

Dave and Harley are given a pot of coffee to start with, followed by two large steak sandwiches and French fries. The waitress also gives them each a bowl of strawberries with whip cream. The agents dig into the food and after lunch receive another pot of coffee with the message that Jason Armstrong will be with them in about twenty minutes. The men discuss how much information they are going to pass on to the senator and his staff at this time and decide that they will just pretend that they are only there to check out the room that the fund raiser will be held in and the route the senator will take getting there. They also decide they will find out who the senators chief security advisor is and will tell him of the threat on Monday giving the senator time to change his plans if he wants but not to tip off Adolf and his crew as to have them change their plans.

With time to kill Harley asks Dave" did you ever get involved in the anti-terror unit? I did some background checks on you when Darius asked for help getting the search warrant." Harley pours another cup of coffee for himself and Dave then continues, "It seems you requested anti-terror twenty years ago when you joined the FBI, which I found strange because twenty years ago there wasn't much concern with terrorism." Dave thinks for a minute as the question brings up painful memories, then answers "I was eighteen, and my parents left me and my baby sister with my aunt as they headed for a European trip that they had always dreamed of. On the third and final week of their trip they were in Spain and they had planned to go to a nice night club with a few of the other couples that they had met on the tour. That night my mom had a terrible headache and just wanted to take a couple of painkillers and go to bed but she insisted that my dad go and have a good time. My mom said my dad didn't want to go but my mom regrettably kept on insisting that he go until he gave in and went. That night at the club a Basque terrorist group set off a large bomb at the club killing over forty people. My dad was one of them. When I was told of the bomb and my dad's fate I was furious but had no idea what to do about it until I watched a Sylvester Stallone movie where he was an anti-terror fighter in the United States. A week after that movie I saw Black Sunday a movie about a terrorist attack at the Super bowl. I took the two movies as some kind of sign and decided that I would take criminology at university then join the FBI. I didn't even know if they had an anti-terror unit or not, but that was now my future no matter what. But I realize I was lucky because I had my dad for eighteen good years but my little sister was only one when he was murdered so she has no memories of him at all. I ended up becoming her father figure. We were so close and still are. I guess you could say that she is the daughter I never had."

Just as Dave finishes telling Harley his story Jason Armstrong walked in. Jason was a toll skinny man that walked with a skip in his step. Dave immediately thought that Jason was probably a little light in the loafers. Jason stood six foot six and only one hundred and seventy pounds. Jason was immaculately dressed with a mauve shirt and white pants. He had long blond hair that was obviously died and brown eyes.

Jason introduces himself to Dave and Harley then Dave takes over saying "Jason we are here to check out the itinerary for Monday's fund raiser. We would like to see the room the speech is going to be held in as well as the route senator Ismail is going to take on his way to the speech. We would also like the name of your chief of security and a list of the workers and guests that are going to be attending'

"No problem at all responds Jason. Then he goes on Randy O'reilly is our head of security, he too is a former FBI agent. I can have a complete list of the guests and staff that will be there on Monday night. As far as those from the hotel and the people that are setting up the room, they I don't know but they have been told to finish up and be out by four o'clock so that we have four hours before the speech to do multiple bomb sweeps and let our security set up."

Dave and Harley are both impressed with the plan but Dave not surprised because he knew Randy Oreilly quite well. Randy was Dave's mentor for his first year on the team before Randy retired. Dave kept in touch with Christmas cards and the odd phone call up until two years ago when Randy's wife died and Randy took off saying he was going to find something to do.

Jason takes Dave and Harley of the convention room and of the senator's route that he will take from his hotel room to the convention room. The route is very direct and Jason explains "That's just the way senator Ismail is he thinks he should always be accessible to the people. It's great for politics but a logistical nightmare for security." Dave and Harley make mental note of the doorways along the way as well as all of the vents that could be used as launching pads for the anthrax.

The convention room is much more intriguing it has eight different points of entry, as well as fifteen different vents for air circulation. A sudden burst of air could disperse fifty pounds of anthrax throughout twenty per cent of the room. Dave starts taking pictures of the room from various locations. When Dave and Harley figure that they have enough information to think things over and make some plans for Monday night.

"Jason when will Randy Oreilly get in town?" asks Dave

"Monday afternoon." answers Jason impatiently now as he wants to be polite but also wants to get to his campaign work.

In a hotel room on the twenty second floor Adolf and Ingrid are in bed after making love and Ingrid says" Thank god, we got out on Thursday or we would have been caught up in that raid." Adolph leans over and kisses Ingrid and replies "Honey that's why we are the best chapter in the country, we are always one step ahead of those idiots in the police. Come Monday night we will be heroes ridding the country of a mongrel politician and most of his top supporters. Take the money away from their kind and they don't have the brains to compensate. It will take those years to find another mongrel politician."

"When will our Germen friends check in?" asks Ingrid.

"They will be here on Saturday night. In lots of time for us to finalize our plans for Monday night." replies Adolph who then kisses Ingrid again before going off to shower.

Adolph comes back to Ingrid who asks "How are we going to get the anthrax distributed?"

"We have secured the balloon contract for the speech. Our friends will fill the balloons in the truck. We are using one hundred each of red white and blue. They will fill each of the white balloons with a half-pound of anthrax, then all balloons will be filled with helium. The white balloons will each have a small charge wired to them. The balloons will be hung up around the convention room. The white ones will be dispersed throughout the room, but at least five will be directly above the stage so that we are sure to get the senator. When the charge is set off the helium will explode causing the anthrax to cover the whole room. We will set off the charge as we take the servants exit out." explains Adolph.

Adolph opens a bottle of peach schnapps and he and Ingrid have a glass each to help settle their nerves and make the time go by faster.

Dave and Harley decide to call it a night and agree to go home and get a good night's sleep. Dave wants to be able to catch Stuart's football game in the morning so he tells Harley" Harley I will call Rasheed and ask him to meet us at the office at noon tomorrow. So good night and try to get a good night's sleep."

"Thanks Dave you get some sleep also. Wish your boy luck in the game tomorrow." replies Harley.

CHAPTER EIGHT

Dave enters the noisy house relatively early for him. It is only six thirty. April is busy in the kitchen cooking Dave's favourite dish, veal scaloppini with scuffed cannelloni. Dave sneaks up from behind on his sister and twists a damp dishtowel to a tight rope then snaps it hard just flicking April's behind making her yelp in surprise. April responds by wetting another dishtowel and twisting it. She flick it at Dave and a dishtowel battle has begun.

Dave and April snap the towels at each other back and forth until Dave's towel hits April in her thigh. April scratches her thigh where the towel hit and starts to fake crying. As Aprils cries louder and her scratch on her leg reddens Dave says "April are you okay?"

"No you brute, you keep forgetting I'm barely a hundred pounds. That really hurt."

Dave felling guilty rushes over to his sister and crouches down to inspect her welt, when April grabs a glass of ice water and dumps it over her brothers head as she bursts into laughter" Dave you will never learn. I've been pulling that act on you since I was a child. You'll never learn."

A dripping wet Dave smiles at his sister in both relief that he didn't hurt her and out of respect for the way she played him so well. As both Dave and April are laughing away in the kitchen Susan and the boys enter the house roaring in laughter. Dave looks up and sees that his wife is completely drenched he can't help but laugh as Susan pretends she's mad at the boys. Dave asks" What the hell happened to you Susan?"

"We were washing my car and the boys thought that it would be funnier if they washed their mom." answers Susan.

"Well the boys were right, but they are too dry." says April as she pulls the spray from the kitchen faucet and turns it on the laughing boys. Susan grabs a towel and wipes the laughing tears from her eyes. Susan then tosses the towel to Dave and says "She's your sister you clean up the mess.' Then looking at April Susan says" April dinner smells great. I'll go to the wine store and grab us a couple of red. I'll be back in fifteen minutes. Do I have time?" April smiles and says "Oh yeah there is always time for wine. Besides dinner will be at least forty five minutes, longer if your husband doesn't get out of the way."

Susan returns from the wine shop with two bottles of red wine just as Aril finishes mixing the Caesar salad. Dave grabs the salad bowl from April and sticks it into the fridge to chill. Dave then says "April you go have a glass of wine with Susan and I'll clean up."

"Oh, oh does this mean you are going to be doing a lot of overtime again? And this is your way of preparing Susan? Dave you guys have been married a long time. Don't you think Susan knows you by now?" Asks April.

"Yeah I know she does. Go have some wine." says Dave smiling at his sister who then spins and happily heads for the wine.

April comes back into the kitchen as Dave washes the pots and says "I hope you are at least going to make it to Stuart's first real football game in the morning. He is looking forward to you being there so much."

"Yes I'm going to the game. It starts at ten and then I will have to leave. I have to be in the office by noon." replies Dave.

After the dinner Stuart and Ryan go to bed early. Stuart all excited about putting his Bills jersey on for the first time in a real game. Susan and April talk into the wee hours of the morning mostly about how a young beautiful woman like April could choose to spend the nights alone.

"The only really good man out there is my brother Susan and you already have him. Besides with my brother there would be a considerable ick factor." Replies April

Susan and April finally finish the bottle of wine and decide that at two thirty in the morning it is time for bed.

At seven thirty on Saturday morning there is a roar in the hall as the adults awaken only to realize that it's just Stuart getting his football uniform on and getting psyched up for his first real football game. Dave Susan and April gather for the early morning rush of caffeine while Stuart and Ryan eat their sugar laced cereal. As April grabs a handful of the sugar treats she says "Well at least we know Stuart will have enough energy at the game after eating a bowl of this crap."

The gang files out and into Susan's minivan to head to the football field. It's a perfect day for a football game. The morning has broken with a high sky and temperatures in the mid-seventies with little or no breeze to effect the ball on kicks or passing.

Susan pulls the van into the parking lot at the park and Stuart grabs his helmet and sprints across the field to the end zone where the team in blue with red and white trim are gathering. At the other end of the field is a team dressed in the green and gold colours of the Green Bay Packers. Dave walks to the kiosk and buys three large coffees for him and the girls and a chocolate milk for Ryan.

The referees gather at centre field and blow the whistle to assemble the team's captains. The Bills win the coin toss and elect to receive the opening kick-off. On the first drive Stuart leads a ground attack that marches the ball all the way down to the Packers twenty yard line. Stuart then runs a brilliant fake reverse and sprints uncontested into the end zone for the touchdown. Stuart completes a short pass for the two point convert. Dave feels a burning pride overtake him as his eldest son leads the Bills to a forty one to ten route of the Packers. Susan and April head to the kiosk and buy large Pepsi's for the whole team.

The boys enjoy watching the second game knowing that they have already won their game and Dave interrupts to have Susan drive him home so that he can make it to the FBI office by noon. April stays behind minding the boys as Ryan keeps tackling her.

Dave arrives at the office and Harley and Rasheed are already there waiting. Harley is drinking a large coffee with another sitting in front of an empty seat obviously for Dave. Rasheed meanwhile is sipping on an extra-large Pepsi.

"What have we got for Monday?" Asks Dave.

"Well we have contacted your old buddy Randy Oreilly and he will meet us at ten o'clock on Monday morning at the coffee shop the Westin hotel" says Harley.

"And I got a picture of the men who were on the plane as crew when your friend friend Rapheal Torres flew in from Germany. Their names are Hans and Frederick Ratchner. Both are known to the Berlin police as neo Nazi organizers." fills in Rasheed as he slurps down his last bit of Pepsi.

"We have a couple of agents circulating at the Westin looking for the four known suspects, but they've had no luck. They could easily be disguised." adds Harley

"Let's get hold of all the security tapes from the hotel to see if we can find any of the suspects in the pictures." suggests Dave.

"Already have a team working on the films in research." says a much more self-assured Rasheed.

"If we have all the extra help checking out the tapes. Let's head back to the hotel this afternoon and set up some more cameras but hide them in vents so that they won't be detected." suggests Dave.

The three men head out to the Westin hotel to pick out the locations for another fifteen surveillance cameras. Once at the hotel Rasheed starts marking the preferred locations for the cameras while Harley and Dave check out what will be Senator Ismail's room on Monday.

The room is on the twenty fourth floor and is massive. "Wow now I understand why some men go into politics. This room is bigger than my apartment." comments Harley. Dave and Harley spend a half hour inspecting every inch of the room but find nothing out of the ordinary, so they decide to gather up Rasheed and relax until they meet Randy Oreilly on Monday morning at ten o'clock.

Dave heads home to an excited and noisy house. Stuart comes running around the corner from the den when he hears his father's voice. "Dad, dad look the coach gave me the team ball for offence. We play the Cowboys next week and they got beat twenty two to six. So they should be easy." Exclaims a still excited Stuart.

"Don't take any team too lightly Stuart. It might also mean the team that beat them is the best team, but you guys played great today. You can tell grandma all about the game tonight. Your mom and I are going out to dinner with Aunt April and a friend." Says Dave.

"Yeah Dad I heard. I think Aunt April would rather stay home and be with us. She's getting better at Packman." intercedes Stuart who has intuitively noticed April's reluctance at going out on tonight's blind date.

April Dave and Susan are waiting in the living room for Tony's arrival. Tony was supposed to be there at seven o'clock but he is now an hour late.

"This is a great first impression." Says April sarcastically to Susan.

"Oh I'm glad you're ready to give Tony a chance tonight. He is a successful gorgeous man April." says Susan trying to convince April to give Tony a fair chance.

The doorbell rings at seven forty five. It's Tony. Tony is a dark tanned strong looking man standing at six feet tall. He is extreme Ely fit and looks about thirty five. Tony has his black hair slicked back and is wearing a white dinner jacket with a black shirt and pink tie. April admits to herself that Tony is good looking, but does not care for his outfit or hair. Tony is introduced to April by Susan and he immediately leers at April up and down. April feels herself being mentally undressed and takes an instant dislike to Tony. April is dressed in a light blue short skirt and a white blouse.

She is wearing three inch high hells that accentuate her shapely legs.

The four jump into Tony's Ford Explorer and head out to dinner. April senses Tony staring at her thighs so she pulls her skirt down further to cover up her legs. April now is wishing that she had worn her slacks instead. At least she is happy she doesn't have too much cleavage to show him. The uncomfortable situation of sitting beside Tony in the front comes to an end temporarily as the vehicle pulls up to the restaurant. April notices that Tony deliberately takes up two parking spots as to protect his car from bumps.

The two couples enter their names on the waiting list and head to the bar for a pre-dinner drink. April is happy to be able to converse again with Dave and Susan. Tony carries the conversation mainly talking about his job as a stock broker and how successful he is with all his toys and properties. Dave is also fed up with all of Tony's self-adulation so he smiles wryly at April and rolls his eyes then says "April did that old boyfriend of yours from high school ever stop calling you or did he finally move to his villa in France." Susan realizing immediately that Dave is making an inside joke directed at Tony's bragging quietly kicks Dave under the table to show her disapproval at Dave's humour. Susan also realizing that her attempt at matchmaking has been a total; disaster tries to give April reprieve by asking "April will you come to the washroom and help me please? I think my dress is catching in my bra maybe you can untangle it." April jumps at the opportunity to get away. At least the evening isn't a total loss as April gets to order her favourite dish of lasagne.

At the table Dave struggles for something to say to a man he has taken a disliking to, so all he can think of is to talk about Stuart's football game from earlier in the day. Dave keeps watch on the women's washroom door hoping for a quick return of Susan and April. April has other ideas as she hopes to delay in the washroom long enough for dinner to have arrived at the table.

"Oh April I'm so sorry. This guy is so good looking I guess I never realized what a dud he really is." Explains a sympathetic Susan.

"Just if we can hurry up and get through dinner I'll be happy. If either you or Dave suggest going out after the meal for a drink I may be forced to beat the both of you up." replies n annoyed April.

"I don't think you have to worry about Dave trying to extending the evening. He doesn't seem to like Tony that much." Explains Susan.

When April and Susan return to the table, Dave seems visibly relieved at their reappearance. Dave reaches over and pulls Susan over and kisses her quickly. Tony liking the idea inappropriately does the same to a shocked April. April luckily moves her head quickly enough to only offer her cheek to Tony.

Dinner finally arrives much to April's relief. April's respite is quickly ended when Tony reaches under the table and places his hand on April's left thigh. April's face goes red immediately and she instinctively tries to pull her leg away from Tony's hand. This only causes Tony to squeeze April's thigh, giving himself a cheap feel.

April is now giving up on the idea of trying to keep the evening civil so she blurts out "Tony do you mind the leg is mine get your hand off." Dave and Susan are startled at first by how loud April was but then by her words as they sink in.

Things don't seem like they could possibly get worse, when Tony proves that theory incorrect by saying in a degrading voice to April "C'mon dear you can't be that naïve I know you must have had a man before. With the entire room listening and watching the drama unfold, April bolts to her feet and grabs her hot lasagne and dumps it over Tony's head. The red sauce immediately stains Tony's white jacket. As Tony's face distorts with anger and embarrassment Dave reaches across the table and roughly grabs Tony's arm as Tony was making a fist in a threatening gesture.

"I think it might be best for you if you just leave Tony." spits out an angry Dave. Tony gets up and storms out again embarrassed as the restaurant patrons all start cheering and applauding as he walks out.

Dave laughs and signals to the waiter "Excuse me the lady seems to have spilled her dinner could we grab another and maybe another round of drinks would be a good idea too, please." suggests Dave. The waiter laughs and says "Sorry for laughing but that guy was a jerk everyone could hear him and thought he was a real jerk. Also who wears a white jacket anymore? Haven't seen one like that since reruns of Miami Vice."

April finally cools down and laughs. "Susan I think this evening is self-explanatory of why you will no longer try and set me up with men."

"Okay April sorry I never realized he was such a jerk but it does explain why he never seems to go out on a second date." Chuckles back Susan.

The three eat their dinners and finish a couple of drinks when Dave reaches for his cell phone and says "I guess its Windy City taxi for our ride home."

Once home the girls grab one more glass of wine as a night cap then head off to bed still laughing about the evening.

CHAPTER NINE

On Monday morning an anxious Dave jumps out of bed early and rushes through the shower and grabs his flak jacket again on his way to the car and takes off quickly for the office. Dave feels a pang of guilt for telling Susan that he is only working routine security all day and evening for the visit by senator Ismail. Dave has neglected to mention that they expect some kind of attempt on the senator's life this evening. Figuring he isn't really positive and also why worry his wife? There is nothing she can do to help anyways. Dave decides he is going to make a point out of bringing in lunch after his meeting with Randy Oreilly. This will allow him to see Susan his boys and April before maybe putting himself in harm's way again.

Dave picks up a couple of large coffees and an extra-large Pepsi for Rasheed. Dave enters the office and sees Harley and Rasheed are ready to go.

"Wait a minute Rasheed you can't go today. You're not a field agent. You can help us from here and keep the research team checking those tapes. Remember that they are probably in disguises now. They're hair can be any length or colour." Explains Dave.

"Yes we have been looking for that but the face recognition program should still be able to get around that. We are taking four stills of everybody we find and running them through the program. Still no luck so far. Hope you guys have better luck then we are." Answers Rasheed.

After they finish their coffees Dave and Harley take off for their meeting with Randy Oreilly. Harley suggests "I think we should maybe try and get the Senator to shut down the fund raiser for tonight. If he reschedules it will at the very least stop this attack and give us more time to locate these suspects."

"Yeah Harley it works in theory but these politicians never seem to want to shut down a scheduled event. It might hurt their appearance of invincibility and bravery. Nothing worse than looking scared to the public" replies Dave.

"But it might end up saving hundreds of innocent lives if he cancels" continues Harley.

"Okay Harley we will try our best but let's bet tomorrows coffee and crispy cream doughnuts on this. I say he will not cancel." Bets Dave. Harley agrees and the two agents leave for the coffee shop at the Westin hotel and their meeting with Randy Oreilly.

When they arrive at the coffee shop Randy Oreilly is already sitting waiting for them, Randy looks up and his face lightens up when he recognizes Dave.

"Dave Gellar you look fabulous if not a few years older. How's that little woman of yours?" asks Randy as he jumps up and rushes over to shake Dave's hand. Randy is a man in his early sixties in incredible condition for his age. Dave wonders if Randy would still be able to take Dave in a fight. Dave's glad they're friends and he will never have to find out. Randy stands at six foot one and a hundred and ninety pounds. Randy's hair is grey in a short crew cut. Looking at him it is obvious that Randy is in the law enforcement business. Dave introduces Randy to Harley and the men sit down. The waiter immediately brings over a fresh pot of coffee. Randy starts "Okay boys what's the scare? The FBI doesn't send in its big guns unless it's something serious."

"Well Randy we were hoping the Senator might call off tonight's speech. We have strong reason to believe that there will be an attempt on his life tonight using anthrax." explains Dave.

"Holy crap! That serious stuff. What's your lead?" exclaims then asks Randy.

"We have the informant who brought in the anthrax and we also found information during a raid on the local Arian Nation branch that points to the senator and tonight's speech. We figure they want to attack the senator because he is the most prominent minority politician in the country." explains Dave.

"Well gentlemen drink up then. Let's go see the senator right away. There's no time to waste." Says a surprised and suddenly adrenaline filled Randy Oreilly.

Randy leads the men upstairs to the senators room and says" Senator these men are with the FBI they would like to have a word with you."

"Senator my name is David Gellar and this is Agent Harley August. We feel we have discovered a serious threat to you for tonight." Says Dave.

"Please gentlemen my name is Akeem and this is my assistant that I understand you've already met, Jason. Okay men spit it out, what seems to be the problem?" asks the senator.

"It seems we have really credible evidence that a group of the Arian Nation will make an attempt on your life tonight senator. And we would wish that you consider postponing your speech." Explains Dave.

"If I postponed a function at every death threat that I get I'd never make an appearance anywhere." responds Senator Ismail.

"Well Senator, I mean Akeem, this one is a little different. What we know for sure is that there is a definite group wanting to kill you. They have been arrested in large numbers, unfortunately the leader got away. We are looking for him and have put many more agents on the case. We will even bring another dozen in tonight. Our problem is that we know they intend on using anthrax in the attack. We feel if you call off the speech, you may be saving a few hundred of your supporters also. As well as giving us some extra time to catch these men and women." reports Harley taking over from Dave.

"Damn! Anthrax, Are you sure? Sorry dumb question of course you're sure. I will talk to the Democratic Party and try to convince them to go along with postponing fund raiser. I will explain that the lives of the contributors have to be saved. They will look at the money that is at risk and probably agree. Money talks in this business, people can be replaced." Blurts out Jason.

"Jason try a little more tact in your distaste for our system. It's always better to change the system from within. Says the senator who then turns to Harley and Dave and continues "Gentlemen Jason and I will try. I can't promise anything for sure. We have people coming in from all over the country.

Senator Ismail calls for the organizers of the evening's dinner and speech to see him immediately in an adjoining private room.

"Gentlemen it seems we have a definite problem with tonight's dinner." Starts the Senator. "The FBI is advising me to postpone tonight's event to q later date, due to a very credible risk for an attack. Not just against me either gentlemen but it seems that the attempt will be made on the whole gathering."

"Senator calling off the dinner would be political suicide. It will seem as if you aren't strong enough to stand up to terrorists if you back off at a threat like this." Pipes in David Levine the Democratic party's top adviser for the evening's events.

"Well we can give the agents until six o'clock to come up with something before making our decision but right now I'm leaning with the agent's advice. We can always say that I took ill from food poisoning or something else. Isn't that the type of advice you guys specialize in?" Says senator Ismail.

"Okay Senator we will gather back here at six thirty then and make our final decision, but Akeem try to think of the consequences if this turns out to be just another hoax." pleads David Levine.

"I just don't want to have the consequences of this being a real attack and us ignoring it. So I will make up my mind after talking to the agents at six." Responds Akeem.

CHAPTER TEN

In the balloon van outside the Westin hotel Adolf, Ingrid and the other two Germen men are filling the carefully prepared balloons with helium gas allowing them to float. This group is only filling the red and blue balloons. The German chemist has already prepared the white balloons with a mixture of anthrax powder and helium gas. He has also attached a small charge inside each balloon with an exposed wire. Hen an electrical charge is set off the charge inside each balloon will ignite the helium gas. This will cause the balloon to explode and the anthrax to be dispersed throughout the ballroom.

"Okay Klaus the red and blue balloons are ready now so you and Ingrid can grab the white balloons in the other van and meet us inside the ballroom. Remember to let Ingrid do all the talking if you get stopped and questioned. Her name is on the passes as one of the owners of the balloon company so it will seem more authentic. Once inside we will install the balloons up high and evenly spread out throughout the ballroom. I will set the ones above the stage myself. Once we are done, I want everybody to hide in the serving kitchen. We won't be detected there. At eight o'clock the speeches will begin so I will detonate the charges at precisely eight ten. Good luck and talk as little as possible." Finishes Adolf in his final address to his fellow members before they carry out the plan.

At six o'clock Dave and Harley find the senator waiting in anticipation for their arrival. As the senator sits quietly contemplating what to do he looks up and says" Please tell me you have a good lead that will prevent any trouble tonight?"

"No senator I'm afraid no. We have neither found the suspects whereabouts or have we enough confidence to believe that they may have left town." explains Dave.

"Senator we both still strongly advice that you quietly postpone tonight's event but Dave and I were thinking that if we could quietly and safely clear the guests outside for a while under a ruse. We might be able to search the rest of the area and direct the people from coming back into the ballroom. This way it will at least look as if the event has been cancelled by the FBI and not by your party. We have arranged for some players from the Chicago Bears to be outside to sign autographs and pose for pictures with the throng of people. As well we are having a temporary bar set up to help entertain your guests." explains Harley.

"Well maybe if my associates and I stick around in the room for a while we can maybe extend the time before the attack allowing the ballroom and the hotel lobby to be evacuated completely without tipping off Adolf and his gang." suggests the senator.

"Senator our first priority is to keep you alive so putting yourself at risk by delaying your departure may not be the wisest answer." Intercedes Harley.

"Well gentlemen it's seven o'clock and the guests will be arriving any second and the ballroom is already to go so I think we have run out of time and options. At seven thirty we will announce that the autograph session has begun and that there will be a complete free bar open in the lobby near the main entrance downstairs. Meanwhile agents will be checking those heading to the bar. Also the senator Jason and Harley will stay visible to the whole room by being near the stage so that the conspirators won't get tipped off by seeing the lobby being evacuated. But senator as soon as the lobby is clear you are out of here also. Lead by a few of our agents. This will allow our forensic team total access inside the ballroom and hotel to search for the anthrax. Explains Dave." The speech is supposed to start at eight o'clock so we thought if we emptied the room for the autographs at a quarter to eight. We will have surprise on our side. We have arranged for three Chicago bears players and two from the Bulls to be signing the pictures in a sealed off area outside. We also have the special permit from the city allowing us to have the bar open outside.

When everybody is outside and safe we will have our forensic team enter through the backrooms wearing protective gear. If there is any anthrax in the room they will discover it. Continued Dave.

"What if the attack is planned for when the guests start arriving?" asks Jason.

"That is a possibility but I am banking on the fact that the real target is the senator. And they will wait for his staff to gather around him. Making the most logical and deadly time for the attack to be shortly after the senator's speech has begun." explains Dave.

"At least that way the lobby will be emptied and if we are stealth enough the suspects will be too busy arranging their attack to notice the hotel is emptying. Once the lobby is empty senator we will exit you and your staff through the servants elevator, then seal the exits and thoroughly check everybody as they try to exit the hotel." adds Harley.

With the speech to start in fifteen minutes Jason calmly takes to the stage and announces, "We have a special surprise waiting for all of you here tonight. We have gathered members of the Chicago Bears, Chicago Bulls, The cubs and the White sox who will all be posing for pictures with you and signing autographs outside until the senator's speech starts. There will also be a complimentary bar open for the guests of the senator to quench your thirst during the pictures. Please be only one hour for we are starting the senator's speech promptly at nine o'clock then we can all enjoy our dinners.

In the back room behind the kitchen Adolf hears the announcement and his heart gives a sudden little jump but he is immediately calmed when he looks into the dining room and sees that the tables are still set and the senator and his staff are going over their notes for the evenings speech. Adolf returns to the back kitchen and informs his team that the plan is still running full steam ahead just that the charges will now be discharged shortly after nine o'clock instead of eight o'clock.

"C'mon people it's a beautiful day outside and the drinks are cold. We are only taking an hour before we start serving the dinner so please enjoy yourself until then and remember the salad and shrimp cocktails will be served promptly in an hour." reports Jason to the remaining few that remain upstairs not having taken advantage of the free bar or meeting the players.

As Jason finishes his short controlled speech, Rasheed rushes to the front entrance quietly getting Dave's attention. Dave proceeds over to Rasheed and the two step into the lobby as to not be detected talking

"Dave we finally received a break and got a positive result from our face recognition program today. It seems Adolf and his girlfriend Ingrid slipped into the bar last night for a night cap. Adolf now has long blond hair, obviously a toupee of some kind and both are likely wearing long sleeves to hide their swastika tattoos" says a hyperventilating Rasheed.

"Great work Rasheed now just try and take a deep breath and relax so that you don't tip off anyone that we may be suspicious. Rasheed give Harley the package with the photos you were able to run off, and he will distribute them throughout the undercover agents here. Then I want you to go outside with the crowd and have a drink. Maybe grab a picture to send to your family while you're out there. The less people we have inside the better our chances of capturing the foursome" explains a grateful Dave.

With Rasheed proud of himself he gladly heads outside to the bar and orders his usual Pepsi. With the room empty the agents then direct their attention to emptying the lobby with great success.

"Geez Dave an offer of a free drink or two will empty any crowd. That lobby was packed with people a minute ago now look, it's practically empty. I think it's time to bring in the forensic team and see if we can end this threat." suggests Harley.

"Yeah Harley you're right but let's herd all the staff outside through the gauntlet of agents and check that they really are who they claim to be. Rasheed gave you those pictures of Adolf and Ingrid and I'm sure they are lingering about in here to get a perverse thrill of the glimpse the aftermath of their plan will cause.

In the back kitchen Adolf and Ingrid are patiently waiting for the hordes of people to return so that they can detonate the balloons and get out fast amongst the confusion. Neither has noticed that their two German friends have already departed as soon as they noticed the mass exodus of people leaving the ballroom. So all that is left are Adolf and Ingrid neither yet realizing that the gig is up on them

A group of agents and police enter the kitchen and the back rooms and start to herd the employees through the hallway and out the backdoor. Suddenly Adolf and Ingrid are consumed by panic as they realize their Germen brethren have made their escape. The remote to ignite the balloons is too far away in a jacket on the far side of the kitchen, for Adolf to get to even if he had the nerve to set off the charges prematurely. Instead Adolf consumed with panic grabs hold of Ingrid's arm and they try and make a run for it. With over thirty police and agents around the pair of Nazi's don't make it very far. Then Adolf makes the fatal mistake of losing all composure and reaches into the sock on his right foot to try and dispose of the gun he is hiding there. A local Sergeant thinking that Adolph's sudden moves and the reaching into his sock are indications that Adolf is about to make a run for it blasting his way out like in the old west. So the officer quickly fires two shots into Adolf's chest collapsing both his lungs. Adolf drops to the floor in a gasping wheezing heap followed closely by a hysterically crying Ingrid.

As the action down the hallway takes place a team of fifty well protected forensic officers enter the ballroom through the back entrance dressed in their chemical outfits and start their detections for any signs of anthrax.

While the team continues to search, Rasheed bursts back into the ballroom yelling, "The balloons, the balloons, check the balloons. We have another positive identification of one of our four subjects as they carried the balloon decorations into the ballroom. So maybe we should start looking there first."

Sure enough as soon as the forensic team starts to check the balloons they discover the wires protruding from each white balloon. When one agent carefully removes one of the white balloons and takes it to the security of the chemical truck in the back parking lot the balloon is burst inside and sure enough there is enough anthrax in this one balloon alone to kill a dozen people. The agent radios in immediately, "We are sending in sealed containers to put all the balloons inside of We have just made a positive identification of anthrax in balloon we removed. So handle all the balloons with extreme caution."

After taking two hours to carefully empty the ballroom of all the balloons and to totally shut down the whole hotel completely so that the disinfecting of the entire hotel of all signs of anthrax can begin.

Outside safely secure in an FBI van senator Ismail and Jason are sipping on some wine left over from the free bar as Dave and Harley partake in a well-earned beer.

"Well gentlemen you sure did a great job tonight, and all week long by breaking up this plot. You can be assured that your superiors will hear how professional and well organized you were throughout the whole operation. According to a couple of the men on the forensic team you guys may well have saved more than five hundred lives tonight with your diligence." commends the senator.

"Thank you senator but we had lots of help from our office staff and a ton of cooperation from your own staff." replies Dave.

"Well gentlemen sleep in tomorrow, you've earned the extra sleep. But at two o'clock I'm having a team of FBI dignitaries join me at your office to give you a special commendation for this work. Don't worry you will also get the full year end treatment at the awards dinner. But Harley tells me Dave that an award tomorrow in front of your boss may be of some special significance. So I'll see you too at two o'clock then." finishes the senator.

CHAPTER ELEVEN

Dave arrives home at eleven o'clock to a very excited household. Stuart greets his dad first and says "Dad I ran for two touchdowns today and threw for another as we beat Seahawks twenty seven to six and Ryan has now qualified for the big all state Packman tournament to be held this Saturday at the Chicago Stadium. He is one of a thousand finalists to qualify from all over the state."

"That's great son I'm proud of both of you." Responds Dave.

"Yeah honey we also saw the news. Something tells me you might have been involved in the middle of all the action tonight at the Westin Hotel." comments Susan.

"Yeah we were there but nobody got hurt except one of the bad guys. So everything went well and I get to sleep in tomorrow for a change so maybe we all can have breakfast tomorrow at the House of Eternal pancakes together and maybe you can see if you can set up April with one of your other friends Susan." adds Dave.

April gives Dave a stare that could stop a grizzly bear in his tracks then says "Breakfast sounds good but one sign of some strange man heading towards our table with purpose and this time everybody will get to wear their food."

"C'mon April just remember to get up on the right side of the bed and we can all enjoy breakfast together before I have to head off and meet the senator at the office by two p. m." Says Dave.

The family all sleeps in and after showering crowd into Susan's van to head off to breakfast together for a rare midweek moment together.

After a huge breakfast of assorted pancakes for the boys and bacon and eggs for the adults, Susan takes the family home. Where Dave rushes into his car after kissing his wife and children good bye. Dave then drives off towards the office and his meeting with the senator and FBI brass. Dave is filled with a feeling of anticipation at the thought of Bill Johnson's face.

Upon his arrival at the office Dave spots Harley outside the main office drinking a coffee and Rasheed is standing nervously beside Harley sipping on his usual large Pepsi. Dave grabs himself a coffee to drink just as Jason steps into the hallway red eyed saying" I think I had a little too much of that wine last night gentlemen so let's get the show on the road please. Before I bleed to death through my eyes. Besides the senator has to be back in Washington by seven o'clock tonight for a vote." On that que Dave, Harley and Rasheed all enter the main office where the whole buildings staff has gathered with the exception of Bill Johnson who is delaying in this office in hopes that his absence won't be noticed. As Dave, Harley and Rasheed turn the corner into the main office they are greeted and embarrassed by a round of applause.

The senator starts off "Gentlemen without your intuition and quick actions today's mood mat be very solemn instead of celebratory. Because hundreds may have perished in that attack not to mention myself so once again please accept my gratitude and thanks. Plus Jack Armstrong from homeland security in Washington is here to brief the three of you on some new information we have received."

Now an even more annoyed Bill Johnson sulks his way back into his office where he closes his door in an attempt to ignore the festivities outside. Outside Bill's office Bill sees James Dubbin the head of the United States new anti-terror federal agency call Dave Gellar into a private room. Bill seethes with contempt for Dave's seemingly meteoric rise in his FBI power ranking.

"Mr. Gellar take a chair please. We picked up some very disturbing information from our Israeli friends a couple of weeks ago. It seems that one of their young female agents, a real computer whiz came upon a transmission seriously threatening an attack on our soil within the next year. The young woman was later found tortured and decapitated so we have to assume the information that she gathered was considered quite sensitive to the local terrorists who tortured her. We are asking that that you apply for a transfer so that we can work you out of the Virginia office along with our most advanced equipment. I realize that this is quite a sudden offer but please discuss this possibility with your family and we can talk again in a week or two." offers Jack.

"So what do you believe the transmission indicates so far?" asks Dave.

"They said in the transmission that it will make nine eleven look like a small accident by comparison and that the plans were already into effect. So we aren't ruling anything out not chemical, biological or even nuclear at this stage. We just know that we want all operatives both foreign and domestic to be on total alert. So Dave if you can help your country in this we will be greatly appreciative." finishes Jack Armstrong as he hands Dave his business card shakes Dave's hand then leaves.

When Dave leaves the office the agents are all still mulling around drinking coffee and eating pastries that were supplied by the senator. Bill Johnson comes out of his office like a wounded bear and hollers "Okay the parties over just because an agent got lucky is no reason for the rest of you to take the day off. We all have work to be done. Knowing that Bill Johnson has no power over him Harley replies loudly "Well Johnson if you had listened more intently to your operatives in the first place like a true leader is supposed to maybe the senator and the executives from Washington might have taken some time to shake your hand and thanked you as well. But after reading my report I just have to gather they will think of me as I do, as nothing more than a desk filling bureaucrat." After Harley's outburst Bill storms back into his office and Harley realizing he may have gone too far heads out of the office and back to his own department.

CHAPTER TWELVE

Its Saturday morning a huge day for the Gellar household as Stuart plays his third football game at ten o'clock. Then Ryan goes to the Chicago Stadium for the big Packman tournament for a two o'clock start and later that evening April will be heading home to Milwaukee to prepare for the new school year.

At the football game Stuart has another standout performance leading his Bills to a thirty two to ten victory over the previously undefeated Saints. Thus solidifying Stuart's teams hold onto first place. When Stuart arrives back at the car, April has purchased Stuart and Ryan both large chocolate milkshakes from the ice cream truck.

"You know April ice cream and milkshakes always taste better when they come from an ice cream truck" comments Susan.

"Well I figure the Packman tournament should be over somewhere around five o'clock. So right after that I better head on back to Milwaukee and get ready for school starting there on Tuesday." Says April as they all load up into the van for the trip to the Chicago Stadium and the state Packman championship.

The parking lots are just starting to fill up for the early rounds of the competition. Ryan senses all the excitement but doesn't quite know how to handle all the people and the noise of the crowd, so he clings to his mother's leg while positioning himself between the safety of his mother's leg and his dad. As they tussle their way to the contestants entrance Ryan starts getting more and more unnerved. But once inside the wide open space of the arena Ryan starts to settle down. He builds into his own comfort level as soon as the first round starts. Ryan is undeterred by the buzzing and ringing music emanating from the game as his first round score decimates his competition. Sending Ryan all the way through to the third round with a bye.

During the one hour break Ryan gets before he has to return for the third round the family all go to the cafeteria where they enjoy the delicacies available at every hockey arena in the country. Old shriveled hot dogs downed with flat cola and for desert stale popcorn. As April and Susan gag their food down, Ryan and Stuart act as though the food is the best meal they have ever tasted.

Although Ryan is by far the youngest competitor to qualify for the tournament, there are still plenty of children of the other competitors running around. Ryan's difficulties communicating with others seems to dissipate in all the excitement as the boys create their own soccer game by rolling up the foil wrapping that the hot dogs came in into a ball shape. Dave and Susan sit in awe at the progress that Ryan seems to have made since Susan uncovered that old toy of Dave's in the basement. As the call goes out for the players to take their stations for round three, the adults take their positions while Stuart grabs another scrumptious hot dog.

This round Ryan has gathered a following to watch him play because his first round score was the highest of the round. The crowd screams and cheers in delight as the flashing ghosts are devoured at a record pace. All the attention finally gets to Ryan as the crowd noise and movements begin to unnerve him. Ryan without warning suddenly stops playing but he has already accumulated the fourth highest score which qualifies him for the final round, which is to start at five o'clock. The tournament organizer Josh Roberts was watching Ryan's round with great interest and was surprised when he noticed Ryan just stop playing for no apparent reason. Josh walks over to Ryan's family quite curious to inquire as to what might have happened. Josh spots April and seeing that she is quite pleasant on the eyes decides to ask her what happened.

"Excuse me can you tell me why the young boy suddenly stopped playing the game in the middle of the round?" asks Josh.

"He is just a twelve year old boy and he suffers from autism. He gets scared by large groups of people. We find this tournament and game to be a major breakthrough for him. By the way I'm just his aunt not his mother. His parents are the two close to him over there. If they are nearby he seems calmer and more at ease. Answers April.

"Well it would be great if Ryan could win the tournament. We really aren't allowed to cheer for any one contestant over the others but if a young autistic child was able to beat all these adults and college students it would be great. So let me see if we can get him on a table that's a little more remote so that the crowd doesn't faze him quite so much." suggests Josh. As the five finalists reach the stage in the middle of the arena, Ryan is placed at a lower level facing a section of the arena that is almost empty. The games are all shown live on the giant screen high above center court. As Ryan comfortably stands at the controls Dave gently tells his son "Okay Ryan your mom and I will be right behind you, okay? Just have fun and when we get home you can beat your Aunt April again and we'll go out for your favorite pizza for dinner."

"Extra pineapple?" asks Ryan

"Triple pineapple promises Dave to his son. Then he continues "Just have fun Ryan."

As a buzz engulfs the audience at the arena Ryan's new atmosphere of being almost in total seclusion has him so relaxed that he starts flying through level after level with only the thought of eating the flashing ghosts in his mind. April looks up at the giant screen and scoreboard and painfully squeezes Susan's arm drawing Susan's attention to the scores. Not only is Ryan leading the final contestants but his score is fifty per cent higher than his closest competitor. Knowing that cheering out loud might only startle Ryan and break his concentration making Ryan look back at his parents and once again stop playing. So the family stays painfully quiet. For April Dave and Susan the last five minutes of the game take a painfully long time to play out. Finally the buzzer goes and Ryan is frustrated to the point of near tears as the games all shut off until Susan arrives and hugs him and says "Honey its okay the time is up y, you just won. You are now the Illinois State champion. In a few minutes that nice man Mr. Josh will be giving you that big trophy."

"C'mon mommy it's so pretty can we put it on top of the fire place mantel?" Asks Ryan no longer upset that the game stopped.

"Honey you can put it anywhere you want to." answers Susan with tears of happiness and joy welling up in her eyes.

After the trophy presentation April runs up to Ryan picking him up and hugging him she looks at Susan and says "Susan you tried to set me up with all those losers when you had the perfect little man fight under your nose." Ryan wipes his cheek in disgust where his aunt has just kissed him. So April says teasingly "If you don't kiss me back young man I'm not giving you any of the pineapple off my piece of pizza." Ryan thinks it over painfully for a minute then reluctantly and gives in and kisses his Aunt April's cheek.

As the six Gellar's drive over to Little Tony's pizza for dinner each dwelling on their own private thoughts. Stuart sitting quietly looking forward to his next football game. April anticipating her the six hour drive ahead of her for her return trip to Milwaukee. Susan beaming with pride and happiness over her son's sudden progress due mainly to the discovery of the video game. Dave has many emotions running through his mind. First is the pride he feels at stopping the anthrax attack, as well as his extreme pride in both his sons and most of all wonderment at how his wife has not only been able to hold the house together while he's put in the extra hours at work. But at how she has been able to turn the boys into two young men and that he realizes his job has made him neglect his part in the child rearing process. Lastly there is the ever smiling Ryan sitting in the car just staring at the huge trophy which he holds in his hands.

As they all pile out of the van Dave noticing Ryan's obvious attachment to the trophy has become an obsession decides to lead the family inside the restaurant leading the way to their favorite table where the trophy proudly becomes the table's centerpiece. Tony a short heavy set white haired man walks over to the table realizing the trophy belongs to one of the boys says, "Wow, now that's a trophy. It's even more impressive than the one the Italians won in eighty two for winning the world cup of soccer. This must be April's trophy right? For winning Miss Wisconsin?" The boys burst into laughter and Stuart showing pride in his little brother says "No Mr. Tony this is the trophy Ryan won for winning the Illinois state Packman championship today. He also won five thousand dollars he can spend any way he wants my mom says and we all get to go to the national championships being held next summer at Disney World.

"Now Ryan maybe I can sponsor you like I do the bowling and hockey teams. So what are your favorite two colors?" asks Tony.

"My favorite color is orange Mr, Tony." answers Ryan

"Okay so I'll have twenty orange t-shirts made up with Little Tony's pizza on the front and the name Gellar on the back. Ryan what is your second favorite color? We can put the lettering in that color." asks Tony.

"Purple would be pretty. Mr. Tony, I would like that." answers Ryan to the roar of laughter from the adults.

"Okay twenty orange and purple t-shirts it is and I'll have each of you made matching satin jackets." finishes Tony.

"Tony that really isn't necessary." protests Dave both out of embarrassment and for the sake of those that might see the outfits.

"It would be an honor for Tony." says Tony in third person. "You've been great customers and more importantly you are my friends." continued Tony.

"So let me guess, a special pizza for the special occasion. Half with pepperoni, bacon and mushrooms. The other half with as much pineapple as I can possibly fit on. Right? And of course a bottle of my best red wine and a pitcher of root beer for the boys finishes Tony ordering for the family.

"Tony that would be just wonderful we all have had such an exciting day today." thanks Susan.

After dinner the Gellar's go home where April after resisting the temptation of the red wine, jumps right into her already loaded up car and kisses and hugs everybody promising to return on Thanksgiving. The family heads on inside while Ryan still clutching to his trophy holding it up so that the whole neighborhood can see. Once inside Susan says "Okay boys time for bed we've had an exciting day."

With the boys safely away for the night Dave enters the den with a glass of red wine for Susan and says "Honey I seem to love you more each day. I am amazed at the job you've done raising our young men." Then Dave adds with a glint in his eye "How about you say me and you head to bed early tonight also." Susan shows her agreement by grabbing Dave's hand and leading him upstairs to their room where once inside she closes and locks the door.

CHAPTER THIRTEEN

TORONTO CANADA

At the Ideal Plumbing warehouse supply in Toronto, sales manager Jim Williams walks into Angus Macpherson's office. Jim is a forty five year old who stands at six foot three and carrying a little extra weight at two hundred and forty five pounds and asks Angus "Will you be ready to leave for Chicago by nine in the morning a week from Tuesday?" Angus is forty three and stands at five foot eleven with short dark curly hair just starting to show signs of turning grey. Angus weighs in at a muscular one hundred and eighty five pounds, but walks with a slight limp in his left leg an after affect from his run in with the bomber in Kabul three years earlier. But this doesn't effect Angus's ability to run much faster than the average man but not as fast as his football days twenty years prior playing football for the Syracuse Orangemen. "Of course I'll be ready, I'm not the one who spends all night every night looking for some tail. The question is will you be on time picking me up?" retorts Angus playfully at his friend and boss.

"Hey I'm the boss here remember. Besides it's better to chase women than sit at home every night like you do since your divorce." says Jim.

"Hey let's not get nasty I'm still recovering from that blood vessel in my brain exploding in my brain in Kabul." replies Angus.

"Good excuse but we're definitely getting you laid in Chicago. Good night and I'll see you tomorrow." says Jim as he leaves Angus's office.

On his way home Angus reflects on the sudden changes his life has taken over the last three years. He was in a safe section in Kabul if there is such a place, or so he thought working for the elite Canadian anti-terrorist squad Joint Task Force Two when a man pushing a hand cart walked right up beside Angus and two British soldiers before detonating a bomb hidden under some groceries in his cart. The blast killed the bomber and the two British soldiers instantly while sending Angus to the hospital for six months of recovery from severe head trauma to be followed by over two years of intense physic therapy. When Angus was well enough to go back to work his wife being tired of Angus's life in anti-terror informed him that she was leaving him and she wanted a divorce. Since then Angus has been on medical leave from his military unit in the anti-terror squad and working as a sales rep for his old high school friend Jim at Ideal Plumbing Supplies. Angus still has trouble sleeping at night due to the nightmares revolving around his experiences in Kabul. Some nights Angus wakes up and swears he can still hear the ringing in his ears and the taste of the blood soaked earth in his mouth. After the cold sweats subside Angus usually gets up for a glass of cold water or on the bad nights a shot of rye and lays awake shaking and staring in the dark until the sun peeps through his blinds and he succumbs to the inevitable day ahead and gets up.

At the Latvian House restaurant in Toronto Alex Krovski and Ivan Yuskavich are meeting to discuss the terror attacks planned to take place in two weeks in Chicago. Ivan is the man in charge of the whole North American operation of the Russian mob syndicate. He is an imposing figure standing at six foot five and weighing two hundred and forty pounds of forty year old steroid induced muscle. Ivan tells Alex "Everything is working as planned The six terrorists have checked in and reported that they are in Rochester Hills Michigan at the safe house just outside of Detroit. And will arrive in Chicago in time for the National Kitchen and Bath show. All the weapons have been delivered to Chicago and will be given to the terrorists, they contain an assortment of machine guns and C 4 plastic explosives."

Alex Trovski replies "Great and plan two has already started so I should be headed back to Afghanistan to follow up with Majid about plan two."

In Rochester Hills the terrorists divide themselves into two groups. The first group consists of two Asian members of Al Qaeda the first is from China and the second is from Indonesia. They are to be given the backpacks with the bombs. These backpacks each contain twenty pounds of plastic explosives and twenty pounds of ball bearings to cause a maximum of casualties due to the projectiles. The four Arab men are from Pakistan, Yemen Saudi Arabia and Syria. They each will be supplied with an automatic machine gun and an explosives bet packed with fifteen pounds of C4 to be strapped around their bodies like a money belt. For now the weapons are being stored in a large wooden chest. They will pack up and leave for Chicago and check in at the Marriot hotel on the weekend before the Bath and Kitchen show. Although the terrorists are well sponsored and have plenty of money they will all check into one room so that they can give each other support. The men will take a low profile spending most of their time in a mosque or their hotel room.

CHAPTER FOURTEEN

TORONTO TUESDAY THE WEEK OF THE SHOW MARCH 31ST

Angus is waiting for Jim to pick him up at his house in Etobicoke in the west end of Toronto. Jim is typically a half hour late arriving. It is a frigid day in Toronto day in Toronto and Angus can't wait for the weather to warm up and the snow to melt. Ever since he was a little boy Angus only enjoyed the snow at Christmas time other than that it just made it harder to play football although he and his friends always managed to play a game of touch football in the snow every year on super bowl Sunday. Jin sequels the tires to a stop in front of Angus's house. As Angus gets in Jim says "I met the nicest woman last night and I couldn't leave her without saying good bye in the morning. Besides this one I want to see again when we get back from Chicago." Angus replies "I hope you use condoms or else half the women in Toronto as well as yourself will be at risk to every sexually transmitted disease that's out there."

The two men head out on the road with no idea of what lays ahead for them. Jim inserts a Grasssroots cd into his player and Angus asks "Just how old are you Jim?"

"You identified the group on the first song so I guess if I'm old you must be to. At least it's better than our old high school team singing Frankie Valli and The Four Seasons in the shower after practice. Now if I start talking about Green Acres or The Rifleman then you can start to complain" Jim fires back.

Jim stops at a gas station just outside Kalamazoo Michigan and Angus heads inside for some gum and to stretch his legs. The store is large and Angus finds his gum and some cheese Pringles and heads back to the car as Jim finishes filling up and heads inside to pay. Jim doesn't notice Angus walking back to the car so he assumes Angus is in the washroom. Jim patiently waits for ten minutes then his patience wears thin and he pounds loudly on the bathroom door and says "Have you fallen in? C'mon we better get back on the road." a strange voice replies with a southern drawl "I'll be out in a minute." Jim realizing it's not Angus turns and rushes out and back to the car where Angus is standing at the passenger side waiting for Jim to get back and unlock the doors. They laugh for a minute and Jim pulls out of the gas station and looks in his rear view mirror and notices a man running behind him holding up his pants in one hand and giving Jim the bird with his other hand. Jim can't make out what the man is saying as Jim and Angus burst into laughter as they get back on the interstate highway.

Angus and Jim arrive at the downtown Marriot hotel in Chicago at six in the evening. They head to their room and Angus grabs a shower. When he comes out there is a note on the desk in the room from Jim saying he's gone to the sports bar in the lobby of the hotel and will wait for Angus there A

Angus gets ready and decides to wear his dark green suit with a bark blue tie that has red, yellow and orange spots on it.

Angus enters the crowded noisy sports bar and immediately sots Jim in conversation with a pretty dark haired waitress so Angus scours the bar looking for an empty seat or stool. He spots an empty stool in the comer of the bar beside a pretty young blond woman just the type Angus has always fallen for physically only to be let down emotionally. The woman is young late twenties he thinks with beautiful blond hair falling just past her shoulders she has an extremely attractive petite frame and as Angus gets closer they make eye contact, Angus's heart seems to skip a beat as he is captivated by a pair of the largest dark green eyes he's ever seen. He finds her eyes almost hypnotic as the stare continues Angus feeling the need to look away embarrassed but can't seem to muster the strength to pull his gaze away. Angus sits down in the stool and orders himself a large draft. Angus saying with his palms sweaty is suddenly startled to a jump as Jim roughly grabs his shoulder and in a boisterous voice exclaims "I think I'll talk to Joyce a bit longer then we will grab some dinner. Angus, have your drinks and dinner charged to the room." Spotting the attractive blond that Angus is sitting beside Jim nods at Angus with a sly smile giving his approval. Before Angus can correct Jim's gutter mind Jim has already darted off back towards his waitress.

As Angus realizes his night is doomed to consist of eating dinner alone and watching sports in his room his thoughts are interrupted by a soft sweet woman's voice who says "My bet is you will be waiting a long time before your friend returns. Those two are looking at a long night ahead. Angus glances over to the woman next to him that is talking trying not to let on that he has been aware of her every little move and sound. Angus also notices that she carries the clean scent of powder and no smell of overpowering perfume. Angus takes a deep breath to muster up his confidence and introduces himself "Hi my name is Angus Macpherson. "April replies with her hand being offered to shake saying "Aptil Gellar. Well Angus what brings you to Chicago?"

"I'm here with my partner Casanova over there for the National Kitchen and Bath show. How about you?"

"I'm here to visit my brother's family. Excuse me please don't take this personally but that's about the ugliest tie I've ever seen Angus. You're children or wife pick it out for you?"

"No children ex-wife and no this was my fashion choice. Besides how could anyone take a comment like that personally?" questions Angus with a smile that lights up his smokey grey blue eyes.

April asks Angus "If you're Canadian then why don't you have an accent?"

"We Canadians don't have an accent eh." responds Angus with added emphasis on the last word for humour. April smiles back at Angus and he fells a rush come over him as April's white teeth and smile light up the entire room.

April's view now scans past Angus and she says "Excuse me for a minute please Angus, there's my brother." Angus feels like he just got punched in the stomach as he concedes to himself that this is likely the last time he will ever see April and takes a rather uncustomary large swig from his beer when he notices that April has returned to her seat. Angus notices that April's brother has accompanied April to the bar and offers him Angus's stool. "No thanks I'll just bring one over from the other side of the bar." says her brother. Angus notices the brother is a rugged six feet tall and likely about two hundred and twenty pounds. He obviously is a police officer Angus determines this by the clothes and shoes he is wearing and the way he is trying to conceal a shoulder harness under his jacket. April says "Angus Macpherson this is my brother Dave Gellar, the FBI officer." Angus and Dave shake hands and Angus is pleased to notice the same last names this along with no ring tells Angus that April is likely unmarried. The two men order a beer and another glass of red wine for April as Dave says "Angus April tells me you are a plumbing salesman from Toronto." Angus nods in agreement as Dave continues "I'm an FBI officer here in Chicago.

"I kind of suspected that from your suit and the gun in your shoulder harness." replies Angus.

"Oh I was kind of hoping it was the masculine air of authority." says Dave hoping for a laugh.

"Will you please excuse me I have to use the facilities." says Angus as he gets up and wonders off to the restroom.

"Dave do me a favor and invite Angus out to dinner with us." asks April of her brother.

"OH April does this mean that you have stopped hating men?" teases Dave.

"I don't hate men just that last guy who was cheating on me with his ex." retorts April. Angus returns to the bar and Dave says "Angus April wants me to ask you to join my wife her and I for dinner tonight. But she has suddenly lost the ability to speak for herself." finishes Dave just as he feels the wrath of April's kick hitting his right shin. Angus turns to a bright red April and asks "Where are you planning on going for dinner? I would love to join you and does your brother always tease you like this?"

"No he is usually much meaner than this but if he doesn't call his wife and tell her he's sorry that he is already an hour late then none of us will get to dinner." Dave jumps up to his feet and grabs his cell phone to head outside and call his wife. Inside the bar Aptil finishes her glass of wine and orders another glass. Angus asks "Where are you planning on going for dinner?"

"I think you mean we don't you Angus? Unless you have changed your mind we are going to a restaurant on the north side of the street where Dave and Susan live called Applebee's.

"Yes I'm still going April and I'm from Toronto not the Orient we also have Applebee's there." replies Angus as Dave returns from his phone call visibly worried and says "okay let's all hurry up before mount saint Susan erupts." April downs her wine and says "Well we know who is not driving don't we." Dave hustles to get the car and drives it around to the front doors of the hotel where April and Angus are waiting. When the car stops Angus opens the front passenger door and holds it for April to get inside. April glances up at Angus and smiles she is both puzzled and appreciative of his manners something she has stopped expecting from men anymore. Angus then climbs into the backseat as Dave pulls away. The drive to pick up Susan is quiet as Dave is obviously tense. Dave pulls into his driveway and disappears into the house as April explains "Susan and Dave have two boys the oldest is fourteen, his name is Stuart the other is twelve and his name is Ryan but unfortunately Ryan is autistic and doesn't take well to strangers well so it is difficult for Dave and Susan to find babysitters to watch the boys so Susan doesn't get a chance to go out much. Don't get me wrong they are both devoted loving parents and when you see Ryan you will see once he gets to know you he is very affectionate. That is why Dave and Susan can only have a sitter for a few hours at a time and one that is used to Ryan and his problems. April climbs into the backseat with Angus to make room for Susan as she approaches the car. Susan is tall at five foot eight and is fit but her two children have left her with a very shapely frame. Susan's hair is dark brown and hangs down to her butt like Chystal Gayles used to. When April does slide into the backseat beside Angus she sits so close that their thighs are touching. Angus says "April your hair smells like peaches that's very nice."

"That's because I use peach scented shampoo." replies April once again impressed by Angus's observation to detail. Dave and Susan enter the car and there is an obvious tension in the air.

Dave pulls up to the front door at Applebee's and lets the others out of the car. Once inside Angus, Aptil and Susan are redirected to the waiting bar for a drink and told there is a forty minute wait for the dining room. Dave arrives to an even frostier reception from Susan, trying to lighten the mood Angus says Susan April says that this is the ugliest tie she has ever seen. What do you think?" Susan looks at the tie and gives a short laugh and then responds "Well April has always had great fashion sense so I will have to definitely agree with her but on the other hand you are still here so even a hideous tie like that isn't a deal breaker."

Dave excuses himself from the table and heads outside where he phones the baby sitter. Once Dave is gone Angus says to the women "I'm sorry we're late Susan, but on the way to the car we ran into my boss and a big customer from back home and I couldn't drag myself away for over an hour." Susan smiles and not totally believing Angus says" That's alright Angus I'm not really mad it's just so rare that we get to go out for dinner like adults, that I was a little disappointed" Susan gets up and leaves headed towards the washroom and April leans over to Angus and says "Well I better note that down for next time." April continues pretending she is writing in a book." Angus Macpherson lies without any trouble at all." April glances up at Angus and loudly asks "What are you grinning about Angus?"

"You said next time." answers Angus still grinning ear to ear.

Susan and Dave arrive back at the table at the same time and Dave says "alright the baby sitter says she can stay for another three hours so we have lots of time"

"Good then you are going to pay her extra for being late then." says Susan jokingly but correct as she orders herself another glass of wine. Dave is pleased to see that Susan seems much more relaxed now and starting to enjoy herself. Dave feels a little better himself now that some of his guilt has subsided. April asks her brother "So Dave how much extra is the sitter going to cost you for those three hours?" Dave playfully kicks his sister under the table in an attempt to shut her up and change the subject. Dave tries to battle back by saying "April I should have known that you would grab a foreigner to be interested in, you've already shot down most of the local men." The sibling spat is prematurely ended by the hostess who says "Gellar party of four your table is ready follow me please." Angus follows behind the gang and checks out April from behind. He's quite impressed until he shifts to embarrass as he notices Susan watching him watch April. Angus's face goes red with embarrassment but Susan just nods at him and smiles. When they reach the table the women sit on one side while the men sit facing them. Susan says while trying to embarrass Angus again "April those slacks really show off your butt wonderfully, don't they Angus?"

"I must say that I have to agree there." responds Angus realizing that agreeing is the best response to the embarrassing situation that Susan is trying to put him in.

The waitress comes over and takes the dinner orders and leaves her hand resting on Angus's shoulder the whole time she takes the order. When she is through and leaves Dave says "Damn Angus are you wearing some special cologne or something? Because these American women just can't keep their hands of you. Can you April?" April raises her hands in the air in a show that she is not touching Angus and playfully kicks her brother under the table. Dave interjects" April if you are trying to play footsy under the table with Angus he is more to the right." April blushes again and Susan decides to try and put an end to the teasing by asking Angus "Angus do you travel much in your business?"

"Not so much in this job no but in my last job I travelled to Afghanistan and Iraq." answers Angus.

"Oh you were a reporter Angus?" asks Susan

"No I was a member of the Canadian anti-terror squad operating in those countries." Answers Angus.

"I didn't know Canada actually had an army." says April jokingly. As the waitress delivers the four Caesar salads as appetizers to the tackle the hungry foursome quietly digs into their food. The main course arrives just as the salads are being finished. April has a plate full of three different types of shrimp. Dave looking at her plate says "They really do mean you are what you eat right shrimp?"

"Well then why are you eating a ham steak then Dave?" Fires back April.

"Okay you two let's have a truce we have to behave in front of our guest." Says Susan trying to put an end to the insult and teasing slugfest.

After the dinner is finished April orders a large fudge sundae loaded down with whipped cream for desert. Angus asks "April you're so small where do you put all the food?"

"She's eaten like that ever since I met her and she is still barely a hundred pounds soaking wet." Adds Susan.

"One hundred and three pounds thank you very much." Replies April with her mouth full to a chorus of laughs from the other three. After April polishes off her sundae and the others finish their coffees Susan says "It's one thirty I think we should get home and let the baby sitter leave." Angus reaches for the cheque and April snatches it from him saying "Angus they don't accept that multi colored monopoly money of yours down here." Dave leaves and retrieves the car and picks up the others at the front door. Angus gets in the backseat and slides to the far side. April gets in the back seat and pushes herself over until she has physically pinned Angus against the far door. Dave looks in the rear view mirror and says" Make sure you leave enough room to get your belt on April. It would look bad if an officer got a ticket for letting his precious little sister ride in his car without her seatbelt on. Dave arrives in his driveway and gets out of the car to walk Susan inside and Susan says "Angus seems like a nice guy and April is due for another shot at romance."

He's alright I guess but nobody will be good enough in my mind for April "interjects Dave.

Back in the car April breaks the long extended silence by asking Angus "How long are you going to be in town Angus?"

"Until Sunday night if you would like to get together again before that I would love to." replies Angus.

"Yeah I would here's my cell number. I thought you'd never get the hint." teases April. A flush of excitement washes over Angus as he realizes that for the first time since he was hospitalized in Kabul a woman is definitely showing interest in him. Dave returns to the car and shines a bright flashlight into the backseat on Angus and April saying "Just checking things seemed too quiet." As Dave enters the driver's seat feeling a bit like a chauffeur and says "Will that be back to the hotel then sir?"

Yes James is Angus's sarcastic reply.

Dave' scar pulls into the Marriot hotel and up to the front door. Dave sits in the car and waits as April walks Angus back to his room. On the way to the elevator April throws a playful hip check at Angus hitting him halfway up his thigh. They get up to Angus's room and not feeling comfortable dating yet Angus bashfully lets the time drift by. After five minutes of awkward silence that feels more like an hour to both of them Angus reaches his right arm around April's small waist and draws her near him and gently kisses her smooth cheek as he gives her a soft hug. A confused yet happy April says "Good night Angus I'll call you tomorrow."

April enters the passenger seat beside Dave looking a bit bewildered and Dave asks "Well was he a gentleman?"

"Not only that but I wonder how Canadians reproduce. I'm sure I was giving him all the signals that I liked him." responds April still quite perplexed.

"Not only were you giving him the go ahead April, I thought I was going to have to rent a room here tonight just to wait for you but after the last guy it should come as a relief that not all men want to jump right into a physical relationship without getting to know the woman first." says Dave trying to keep his sisters spirits up then he adds "The way he was looking at you it was easy to tell that he was extremely interested, but maybe he has been burned himself before and wants to make sure himself. Besides as your older brother I like it when a man shows restraint with my little sister."

Inside the hotel room Jim thunders "Well Angus did you score? Or do I still have my work cut out for me?" Angus turns on the light and replies "Well I needn't ask you what you did." as he holds up a bra that was lying on the floor besides Jim's bed.

"Well details Angus I want details." razes Jim

"In the words of the Rolling Stones Jim You can't always get what you want. And first of all I don't brag about my conquests and secondly if I did there would be nothing to brag about anyways other than I met a beautiful enticing young woman tonight and I think I'll be seeing her again tomorrow." finishes Angus as he turns out the light signaling the end to all questions tonight about April

CHAPTER FIFTEEN

DAY 2 IN CHICAGO WEDNESDAY APRIL 1ST

In their hotel room at the Chicago Marriot the terrorists are having a meeting.

Ahmad their leader explains the plans for Friday. Opening a large wooden chest that they carried up to their room an hour earlier under the darkness of night. Ahmad reaches inside the crate and pulls out two heavy back packs and hands them to the Chinese and Indonesian men explaining "Inside are the bombs for the attack at the McCormack center. Make sure the first bomb blast in in the coffee bat at seven thirty P.M. our benefactor has arranged a meeting at that time between the mob bosses from Chicago, New York, and Miami here are their pictures. They must be killed in the first blast, there is usually a large crowd gathered in that area and we should be able to kill a lot of bystanders. The second bomb is to explode at the main entrance when the lobby is full of people panicking to leave the building after they here the first bomb.

Ahmad then pulls out four money belts and four AK 47 machine guns out of the chest and keeps one of each for himself then hands one of each to each of the other three Arab men. "These are to be used in the restaurant attack. Our Armenian friend will be meeting with three Japanese men who are from the Yukuza which is the name for the Japanese organized crime syndicate. When the

Armenian man leaves the table to make a phone call, that is our signal for the two of us to open fire on the Japanese men killing them first then we will open fire on the restaurant staff and patrons. The money belts contain fifteen pounds of C4 plastic explosives, these are to be set off after we run out of ammunition for our guns. Ahmad tales a drink out of his water bottle and says "Tap water isn't good enough for Americans yet they blow up our water treatment plants in Iraq so that nobody can even have tap water safely. Are there any questions? The Chinese terrorist asks "where did we get the C4 explosives from?"

"The explosives were stolen from a demolition company in Las Vegas and a hundred pounds were transported here by our Armenian brothers" Explains Ahmad. And with the plans explained the six terrorists set out for a local mosque then dinner.

In Toronto Ivan Yuskavich is talking to his accomplice and lawyer Valeri Yashin. Ivan says "In two days we will have ridden ourselves of the crime bosses from Chicago, Miami and New York allowing our empire to capture the main drug distribution centers in the United States. Also we will have killed the top members of the Yukuza who are in charge of the white slave sex trade in Thailand and Taiwan."

"We should have had controlling share in the slave trade brothels anyways because we supply more than ninety per cent of the women working in the brothels by kidnapping them from former east block nations and smuggling them into the Orient.

At the hotel Jim and Angus grab breakfast in the hotel coffee shop. Jim asks Angus "Do places like this spell their name The Coffee Shoppe so that patrons won't realize they are spending more for the extra p in their name?"

"Did that question keep you awake all night Jim?" answers Angus with a question.

"No I just thought I'd practice being the smartest person in the room for a change." answers Jim.

"Jim when you are alone in the shower is the only time you are the smartest person in the room." insults Angus to a pretend hurt looking Jim.

"Oh nice Angus thanks a lot." retorts Jim

Angus and Jim eat breakfast or in Angus's case he drinks breakfast having three cups of coffee Jim says "Well Angus why don't you just go and call her before you develop an ulcer. Angus heads to the lobby and phones April who still is a little sleepy but happy to hear from Angus. Angus says good morning April can I take you to dinner tonight and a blue's club afterwards for dancing?"

"No but I can take you through seeing I grew up in this city and have a car to drive you, as long as your male ego will survive being picked up by a woman. But you can still treat me if that will make you feel better." replies April with a giggle.

"Very well then how about picking me up at seven thirty so that Jim and I can have time to check out the booths being put up at the show and get an idea of who is in town yet?" asks Angus with his heart racing with excitement at the thought of another evening with April.

"Sounds good to me and I'll pick out the restaurant and the club." says April taking back the lead.

Angus locates Jim back in the sports bar where Angus says "Jim isn't it a bit early to start drinking?"

"Funny Angus I just thought if you were going out with that pretty blond number you met last night I would check out and see if Joyce has the night off work tonight and luckily they said she is, so I'm going to her and try to make plans for myself tonight."

April calls Dave at work and says "Dave I can't make it for dinner tonight because I'm going dining and dancing with Angus but if you are available for lunch I can meet you at Oliver's for lunch at one o'clock."

"Okay April sounds good. Well at least you don't have to worry whether or not Angus likes you anymore, he sure didn't waste any time asking you out again." replies Dave.

Dave hangs up the phone and heads to the FBI's research department where he finds Rasheed and asks "Rasheed can you run me a brief bio check on a Canadian named Angus Macpherson? H Here are all the details I know about him."

"Oh good another terror suspect?" asks Rasheem.

"No just a new interest of my little sisters." answers Dave.

"Damn Dave you know there are going to be a lot of disappointed agents around that were hoping to ask her out once she started dating again." Replies Rasheed with a grin.

"Yes please Rasheed and I had no warning she was thinking of dating again." says Dave relieved that he doesn't have to try and set up April with any of the agents especially after the disasters that happened last summer when Susan tried to set April up.

Back at the hotel Jim and Angus are waiting on a cab to pick them up and drive them to a luncheon put on by American Standard when Jim asks "Okay Angus what makes this girl so interesting since you haven't been on a date since your brain got scrambled in Afghanistan and I know Tina at the office has been trying to get your attention since you started with us."

"I don't know other than I find her extremely attractive physically and she is so easy to talk to and joke around with." answers Angus a little too seriously.

"Oh Angus you have given this a lot of thought, to steal a word from Thumper in Bambi I think you are *twiterpate.*" Angus laughs "There you go again Jim trying to impress me by quoting all the literary greats. But I am surprised I thought the only Bambi's you knew were the ones in pornos."

On his way to meet his sister for lunch Dave picks up Angus's biography from Rasheed. Dave arrives at Oliver's and April is already waiting at a table. Dave sits down and says "April I did a check on Angus's background while I was at the office this morning."

Why Dave don't you trust my judgement in men?" asks April.

"Why no I don't April. Your track record hasn't been that impressive at least not until now but from your attitude I gather you don't want to see the report." says Dave teasingly holding out the report then drawing it back.

"Well if you've gone to all the trouble I guess I should at least scan through it." Says April as she snatches the report out of Dave's hands.

Angus Macpherson is a forty three year old. Born a Canadian of Scottish decent in Toronto. Angus won a football scholarship to Syracuse university where he played as a starter all four years making the all big east team as both a safety and a kick returner in both his junior and senior years. Angus majored in philosophy and literature ranging from Shakespeare to Russian literature. Angus moved back to Canada after he graduated and joined the RCMP as a anti-terror agent after an unsuccessful attempt at pro football in the Canadian Football League. He then switched to the elite Joint Task Force Two when the government put the anti-terrorist duties under the military command. Angus served in Iraq in nineteen ninety one as a sniper then again in Afghanistan in two thousand and two and two thousand and three where he suffered a severe brain injury Dave has added in hand writing (April this explains his attraction to you.) April kicks Dave in the shin under the table at this point then continues to read upon returning home Angus's wife of eight years left him and ever since Angus has been enduring intense physical therapy and has surpassed even the most optimistic outlooks. Since then he has been working as a plumbing salesman for an old high school buddy for the last year.

April finishes the report and Dave says April you look disappointed that the report doesn't say he's a criminal or animal hater in fact he even owns a small poodle back home."

"No Dave I like the report very much but now I feel guilty for reading it. It's almost like I was spying on him." confesses April.

"What do you mean almost like spying on him? April it's exactly what you are doing." says Dave with a laugh.

"Thanks Dave you always know just the right thing to say when I feel guilty." replies April sarcastically.

"April you know in my mind no man will ever be good enough for you. But at least this one comes close." finishes Dave as he heads to the counter to pay the bill.

Angus walks up to Jim at five o'clock and says" Jim I'm going to grab a cab back to the hotel and grab a shower."

"Okay Angus and remember if you get lucky tonight I'm going to waive your curfew." says Jim wryly.

"Thanks dad and you remember to try not to grab any of the models here you already have someone waiting for you back at the hotel and we still need American Standard as a supplier." Warns Angus

Angus arrives back at the Marriot hotel at six o'clock and grabs a shower and shave. He picks out a black suit and his lucky purple tie to wear. Angus heads downstairs early bubbling with anticipation and doesn't bother to look around until he feels somebody bump into him from behind. Angus turns around and his heart skips a beat when he sees that the clumsy person that bumped into him is in fact April pretending to accidentally bump into him. "April you're early." states a surprised and happy Angus grinning.

"Well so are you Angus and nice tie." compliments April.

"Are you being serious?" asks a dubious Angus.

"Yeah I'm serious that really is a nice tie I would never have guessed that you would own such a nice tie after seeing the one you wore last night." replies April her tone dripping with sarcasm.

For the first time Angus is able to pause and look April over. She looks stunning wearing a short black skirt that hems eight inches above her knees and a soft white angora sweater that clings tightly to her petite body and tonight Angus is able to notice that April's chest although not large is ample enough for his tastes. April's hair is tied up with a black ribbon tied into a bow exenterating April's long thin neck. Angus can't take his eyes off of April's huge emerald green eyes. Feeling embarrassed April asks "So do I meet with your approval?"

"April you are absolutely breathtaking that's why I can't speak." responds Angus feeling the embarrassment switch to him.

"Good answer." states April.

Angus grabs April by the hand and they walk together to April's car. April drives to the blues club for dinner and says "This place is hard to get into its blues and jazz that's why I was early. What's you excuse?"

"I was just excited to be seeing you so I couldn't wait." says Angus

"That's nice Angus even if it is a little bit sickening." responds April then she continues "Seriously as I was saying the food here is terrific and the house band plays some really good old motown music as well as swing and jazz from the forties."

It's only seven o'clock so April and Angus go to the clubs bar for a drink before dinner. At the bar April confesses "Angus, Dave did a background check on you and I read it I'm sorry I hope you're not mad."

"No not at all April I have nothing to hide and besides I think it's kind of sweet to have your older brother looking out for you." Answers Angus.

"You know Angus you and Dave have a lot in common, you worked in an anti-terrorist job in Canada and Dave's job with the FBI is on the anti-terror unit." informs April.

April and Angus get called for dinner and April orders a bottle of red wine to which Angus jokes "You know April I'm allergic to red wine so you better drink the whole thing. April looks horrified and Angus adds "Just kidding April drink what you want and we will take a cab back to your brothers or I will drive if you can give directions and I will get a cab from there." April nods in agreement and relief and says Angus try the twenty for once t-bone steak it's the house specialty here." Angus only drinks one glass of wine from the bottle leaving it up to April to drink the rest. As soon as the finish dinner and the tables cleared the band starts to play. When Angus finally grabs April's hand to dance they hit the floor and don't sit down again. When there is a slow song Angus towers over April and he loves the soft feel of the angora sweater and the scent of baby powder and peach shampoo that radiates from April as they dance. April snuggles her head into Angus's chest. When the music finally stops. Angus grabs April her black leather coat from the coat check and buys a long stem rose from the rose lady, That Angus suspects is probably working for reverend Sung Yung Moon or some other religious cult. Angus grabs April by the hand and they walk to the car. The air outside is cold but Angus and April are still hot from all the dancing. Angus opens the car door for April and on their way to Dave and Susan's April phones a cab with her cell phone so that it is there for Angus when they arrive or shortly after.

When they reach the house the cab is already there so Angus walks over to the cabbie and asks him to run the meter while he says good night to April. At the door April asks "Angus you're a good dancer where did you learn how to dance like that?"

"When I was younger my sister and I took disco dance lessons and the moves of swing and jazz dancing are pretty much all the same." answers Angus.

This time Angus doesn't wait for the awkward silence to creep in and take control so he reaches out and grabs both of April's hands and draws her near to him and gives her a tight hug. Then he tilts her head up and kisses her passionately. As Angus turns to leave April grabs his arm and spins him around saying" Not so fast Angus you haven't been dismissed."

"Oh Miss Gellar is that your teachers voice that I detect?" Angus teases playfully. April kisses Angus and they kiss for ten minutes before April says Good night Angus you better go before I make you spend the night or the cab leaves. I'll call you tomorrow Angus." Angus looks lovingly into her deep green eyes one more time and kisses her quickly before finally letting go and heading off towards the cab only to look back and wave at April who was waiting just for that wave.

CHAPTER SIXTEEN

DAY 3 IN CHICAGO THURSDAY APRIL 2ND

Jim and Angus rise early and grab a healthy breakfast of coffee. Jim takes a drink out of his coffee and says "I think we should head to the McCormack center by ten o'clock so we can check on the booths and exhibitors as they put up their booths and get an early start on making contacts."

"God Jim I don't know how you do it, staying out so late every night and still be ready to work in the morning. I was out until two last night and all I drank was one glass of wine and I'm dead tired today. So I think I'll grab another coffee." yawns Angus.

"Get me another cup please also Angus extra cream. Oh and by the way, how did it go last night?" asks Jim.

"It was great and I think you're right April does have me under some kind of a spell. All we did was dance all night before you ask, as if I'd tell you anyways." replies Angus who just with thinking about April feels a rush of energy rush through his body stronger than any coffee ever could.

Angus and Save arrive at the McCormack center and Angus asks "Jim I'm going to head over to grab another cup of coffee, do you want one also?"

"Yeah please Angus a large with extra cream only please and I'll wait for you over at the Kohler booth." answers Jim.

Angus meanders through the maze of boxes and fork trucks towards the coffee bar when he spots a booth of high end quality faucets that he has never seen before. Angus changes an oncoming fork truck and heads towards the faucet booth. While he approaches the four men in the booth don't notice Angus coming and they continue their discussion. S Angus enters earshot of the men he is surprised to hear the men are speaking Arabic, A language he recognizes from his tours of duty in Afghanistan and Iraq. Angus startles the men when he says "Hello." The four men immediately switch their language of speech to English as Angus continues "These are real nice faucets can I have some literature or a card?" A tall man responds "No sir we are just here to install the booth."

"I'm sorry sir my partner is a little gruff this morning can I answer your questions?" asks a slight man dressed in a better suit not wanting to be rude and draw attention to themselves.

Angus sticks his hand out to shake the friendlier man's hand and says "Hi my name is Angus Macpherson, I'm her from Toronto, and do you have any distributors in Canada?

"Not that I am aware of Angus. My name is Jim Cirone and we are the distributors for the United States of America." responds the friendly Arab and Angus finds it strange that call the states by the full name but shrugs it off and asks while checking out a shower faucet "What is the flow rate of your thermostatic mixer and what are the inlet sizes.?" Joe looks confused but answers "The flow rate is very good and the size of the inlets are three." Angus realizes the man either doesn't understand the question or doesn't know plumbing so he looks around some more then asks "What finishes are your faucets available in? and may I have your business card?" the man hands Angus his card and Angus continues now a little suspicious "One more question please, What about the availability of brushed nickel?" the man continues playing the role "No but we will have brushed nickel soon." This is strange because the shower faucet that they are looking at is in brushed nickel. And it is prominently displayed throughout the booth. Angus says "Thanks for the time" and shakes the man's hand. As he heads towards the coffee bar Angus takes out his cell phone and dials the number on Joe Cirrone's business card. A women on the other end of the line answers "Armenian auto sales."

"May I speak with Joe Cirrone please?" asks Angus

"I'm sorry but there is nobody here by that name.

"Oh I'm sorry I forgot he said he would be at the kitchen and bath show this week." says Angus persistently trying to gather as much information as he can. Once again the lady responds "I'm sorry sir but this company sells cars not plumbing so I guess you must have the wrong number." Angus now grows very suspicious and grabs his and Jim's coffees. On his way back to Jim at the Kohler booth he once again walks close to the men and he observes that they are once again speaking Arabic and still not working on the booth. Angus's spider sense kicks in and he decides to phone Dave Gellar at his FBI office.

"Dave Gellar speaking." Dave answers the phone.

Hi Dave its Angus, last night April mentioned you work in anti-terror at the FBI so I thought I should give you a call. I may be over reacting here but I'm at the McCormack center watching the exhibitors set up their booths and I met some Arabic men who said they were Italian but they knew nothing about the product and when I phoned the number on the business card one handed me I got a car dealership in Florida that's never heard of the men. Maybe my stint in anti-terrorism in Canada has made me has made me too suspicious of people but Dave my spider sense is tingling."

"Did you say spider sense Angus? No wonder my sister likes you read the same comic books as her grade five students. Stay there though I'll be right over so I'll call you when I arrive. I'm like you, though I don't think in our positions you can ever be too suspicious." says Dave.

Angus's hangs up the phone just as he reaches the Kohler booth and hands Jim his coffee.

"Yuck! Angus this coffee is cold." says Jim as he reheats his coffee in the microwave at the Kohler kitchen display. Jim continues "What happened Angus you get lost?"

"No I stopped at a booth that has some really nice faucets and they need a distributor in Canada so maybe we should drop by and say hello there early tomorrow." answers Angus.

Angus's phone rings and he and he walks away from Jim for some privacy when he returns Jim asks, "Who was that? April?

"No it was her brother Dave." answers Angus.

"So you signed up for the family package did you Angus?" teases Dave.

"No but I have to leave with him for about a half hour or so. But I'll explain it all to you later." explains Angus.

Dave arrives at the Kohler booth and says hello to Jim. When Dave and Angus head off towards the both that Angus is suspicious of Dave says "When we get to the booth Angus don't let the men see you while I take pictures of the men from another booth hopefully without them noticing me." Angus look son from a booth far away so that the Arab men in the booth don't notice him but Angus is disappointed when he notices that only two of the men remain in the booth. Dave finishes taking the pictures of the remaining two men and signals Angus to follow him. Angus follows Dave into the coffee bar where Dave says "I'm going to the office and have research do a search on these two men anyways."

"Well I hope they do a better search on them then they did on me yesterday your sister didn't get any of the bad stuff." An embarrassed Dave responds "Oh April told you about that did her?"

"Yeah she did but don't worry I have nothing to hide and I think it's rather cute that her big brother still watches out for her." Dave desperately wants to change the subject says "I will call you this afternoon with the results of the search Angus and thanks for keeping an eye out.

Angus finally locates Jim at two o'clock in the Delta booth. Jim pulls Angus aside and asks "Okay now I want to know what's going on. I kind of get nervous when a former anti-terror agent and an FBI agent get together and disappear at a show for about two hours."

"Don't worry Jim nothing is imminent and I will fill you in, in depth tonight." reassures Angus.

Dave phones Angus on his cell phone at three thirty and says "Angus I just got back the report on the two men that I was able to get the pictures of. One man is a Saudi national and the other is a Yemeni national both are in the country legally on temporary visas. Neither man is on any suspect list and they have been watched a little in Detroit at least enough to know that neither is working in the plumbing field so we are going to have the men followed a bit while they are in town but as of now there is nothing too suspicious other than your so called spider sense. Oh and by the way Angus thanks for the lead and in return I thought I should warn you that that April is going to drop by on you tonight at the hotel so act surprised when you see her."

On their way back to the hotel from the McCormack center Angus tells Jim "Dave told me that April is going to come by the hotel tonight to surprise me and that they are going to follow the men that I was suspicious of so for now everything is under control.

"Hey what a minute. What men? And what exactly is under control? Asks Jim emotionally

"Oh those were the men I told you about in the faucet booth. Well they kind of bothered me but Dave did a security check on them and there was nothing too suspicious to raise the alarm but they are going to be followed while they are at the show anyways. Things like this happen every day Jim, and not one thing has gone wrong since nine eleven." explains Angus.

"That's a relief Angus. I'm going to meet Joyce in the bar tonight while she's working so if you're busy in the room with April just make sure you remember to hang out the do not disturb sign." teases Jim with a sly smile and a wink.

"Jim unlike you we are not all controlled by our hormones." replies Angus sarcastically. Angus and Jim get ready for their evening dates in their room. Angus puts on a casual orange Syracuse university sweat shirt and a pair of dark blue dress pants. Jim is ready first and says "bye." as he heads out the door and then to the elevator to take him to the lobby and Joyce's sports bar. Jim looks into the lobby as he exits the elevator and spots Dave drinking a coffee so you does a one eighty and rushes back to the room to tell Angus that Dave is in the lobby. Jim realizes in the elevator on the way back that his heart is racing and that deep down Angus's reassurance that everything was under control no longer seems to be as reassuring

Angus is surprised to see Jim and notices that he seems to have an extra jolt of adrenaline in his system now and asks "What happened Jim did Joyce blow you off already?"

"No you smartass. I just thought I'd tell you your friend Dave is sitting in the lobby sitting in a chair and drinking a coffee."

answers Jim. Angus jumps up and rushes downstairs to see what's up and notices that his quick reaction has startled Jim who now has a worried look on his face. Once downstairs Angus notices that Dave is sitting and watching the four Arabic men that Angus had seen at the show earlier. Angus stays out of the view of the Arabic men but in the view of Dave until Dave spots him and signals to Angus that he has seen him. Angus signals that he will go to the coffee shop and wait for Dave there. From his seat in the coffee shop Angus is also able to observe the four men as they leave and head towards the elevators. Angus positions himself to see the men but they don't notice him. Angus watches as the men enter the elevator alone and it heads upstairs stopping only once on the fourteenth floor then he waits until it returns again stopping only once on it's way at the seventh floor. When the elevator returns to the lobby only one man and his young daughter get off so Angus concludes that the men must have gotten off on the fourteenth floor. Angus returns to his seat in the coffee shop. Dave enters the coffee shop and spots Angus and sits at the same table then Dave says "Angus you know that many coffees a day is going to kill you."

"Yeah, Yeah what the hell are you doing here spying on those Arabic men or following April and I when she gets here?"

"Well I guess I trusted your instincts a little more than my superior did so I had the report from the two agents that they followed the Arabic men to this hotel where I decided to come over for myself. I'm glad I did because I was able to get pictures of the other two men and I've recalled the team and upped the surveillance on them so if they decide to go anywhere tonight the team will be here to follow them. I wish I knew what room they are in." finishes Dave.

"Well I don't know what room they are in but I'm pretty sure that they are on the fourteenth floor at least that's where their elevator stopped." replies Angus.

"You really are an observant one aren't you Angus?" asks Dave in a complimentary tone.

"No just I've learned to become paranoid I guess." says Angus.

Dave uses his cell phone to mail the pictures he has taken of the other two men to the office and tells Angus "I should get a report back on the two men within a couple of hours."

April skips through the lobby door and stops suddenly when she sees her brother and Angus together in the lobby now talking. She continues again and kisses Angus quickly on the lips then she kisses her brother on the cheek. She sounds a little upset when she says "Dave why are you here? I thought you liked the report you did on Angus."

"He is here on official business April, I called him today because I was a little suspicious of a few men that were hanging around at the show today." says Angus hoping to lighten up April's mood but it has the reverse effect because now April directs her attack at Angus. "Oh no don't tell me that you're not suspicious of everybody you see also?" Angus puts his arms around April and hugs her remembering that April's visit was supposed to be a surprise he awkwardly says "April what are you doing here? I thought you were busy tonight."

"Cut the crap out Angus obviously Dave told you that I was coming by." April spits out as her anger takes control.

"Yeah he did April but I'm really glad you did even if it's going to take me a little while to work my way back into your good books." replies a defensive Angus desperate to work his way back into April's good books and hoping for a quick change in her mood.

"I'm sorry Angus but I was just surprised to see Dave here and a little upset that I didn't surprise you and don't try to say something nice now because it's not going to work. But I'll settle down after Dave leaves I'm really directing my hostility at him for telling you that I was coming." finishes April. Dave says good night and says to Angus "Can you call me in the morning I would like you to check out that booth in the morning at the show." Angus nods at Dave in agreement and Dave leaves.

April looks deeply into Angus's eyes and trying to lighten the mood up says "Maybe I was wrong about your tasteful fashion sense last night. I mean an orange sweatshirt Angus just what were you thinking?"

"Hey these are my school colors." realizing that it's April second Angus says "April is today your birthday by any chance?"

"Why do you ask Angus?" answers April with a question to what she finds an odd question.

"Well your name is April so I figured you were born sometime in April." answers Angus

"No I was born on January ninth. My parents named me after my grandmother Gellar." yen April adds "Angus why don't we just go to your room tonight and order in room service and rent a movie tonight?"

"Why don't we eat in the hotel restaurant and grab a cab to the movie theatre," Answers Angus also with a question.

"Why Angus Macpherson are you scared to be alone with me?" asks April dripping with sarcasm.

"No April I am quite looking forward to that occasion at least I was until I witnessed the wrath of Gellar earlier tonight." responds Angus fighting back with sarcasm of his own.

"Okay you win but let's grab dinner now because I'm hungry and the movies start in an hour and a half." says April.

April and Angus both have steak dinners and when they are finished Angus says "If I keep eating like I have this week I'm going to gain fifty pounds. April how is it you eat so much and stay so petite?"

"I guess I have a fast metabolism." answers April.

Angus and April hail a cab after dinner and Angus notices the four Arabic men from the show climbing into another cab. As the cab pulls away Angus notices a black SUV start up and follow them. Inside the SUV are two men dressed in suits and Angus realizes that they must be the FBI surveillance team.

The stakeout team follow the cab to a mosque and wait as the men enter the mosque. When the men exit the mosque they are accompanied by two Asian men who the agents take pictures of and e-mail the pictures back to the research department at the FBI headquarters. The stakeout team notice that the Asian men take a cab in one direction and the four Arabic men head in the other direction back towards the hotel. The agents follow the cab containing the Arabic men and upon their return to the hotel the suspects head straight back upstairs followed by the agents who notice that they enter room fourteen hundred and eight.

Q At the theatre Angus walks over to the candy bar and orders two large Pepsi that come in massive containers and a giant tub of popcorn with topping. When he returns to April Angus says "When I was a teenager I worked at the Westwood theatres and we used real butter ion the popcorn not this topping crap."

"Well I bet way, way back then they didn't have gallon sized soda pop." says April as she pretends to have trouble lifting her cup to her mouth to take a sip of.

"A gallon you mean four liters, remember I'm Canadian" Jokes Angus.

Once inside the theatre when the trailers start Angus grabs hold of April's hand and April reciprocates by resting her head on Angus's shoulder.

When the movie is over Angus and April grab a cab back to the hotel where April walks Angus over to the elevators and pulls Angus close to her where they share a very public and passionate kiss good night. Angus standing in the elevator in a much exited state watches as April meanders back across the lobby on her way back to her car.

CHAPTER SEVENTEEN

DAY 4 IN CHICAGO FRIDAY APRIL 3RD

Dave wakes up early after the disturbing news he got the night before from Rasheed who was working the night shift in research. Rasheed was able to find the identities on the two Arabic men and the Syrian man he identified had been previously put on the FBI watch list as a man with connections to a terrorist group in Lebanon. Rasheed was unable to locate the information on the other man other than that he is an Egyptian national that has been living in the Detroit area also. Rasheed is also able to inform Dave about the two Asian men that the agents were able to snap pictures of Thursday night. The men are from China and Indonesia in the country on temporary work visa and have a booth at the kitchen and bath show called Pure Ceramics. Although these men have a legitimist reason to be in town, Dave still gets suspicious that they are at the same mosque and meeting the suspects from the Arabic companies. Dave has decided to head into the office early and make a formal request for agents to attend the kitchen and bath show to keep an eye on the Asian men and to look for the Arabic men.

Dave arrives at the office at seven o'clock and spots Rasheed still there working so he heads over to say good morning to his young friend. Noticing at Rasheed's desk are four empty tins of Pepsi

Dave says "Good morning Rasheed. You do know that you can get addicted to cola with all that caffeine inside?"

"Yeah Dave I know and you're one to talk with all that coffee you drink."

"Well Rasheed the man my sister is interested in now makes me look like an amateur when it comes to drinking coffee."

"Wow he must really be wired all day then. Dave I kept checking on those Arabic and Asian men all night but I couldn't get any new information on them. I thought with the time difference either our embassies in their countries might know more. I even checked with all our known informants but still came up empty. Sorry." explains Rasheed.

"Geez Rasheed one thing I can definitely say about you is that you are thorough." compliments Dave.

Dave leaves Rasheed as soon as he spots Bill Johnson entering his office. On his way to his bosses office Dave chuckles to himself when he notices Rasheed at the pop machine getting himself another Pepsi.

Q as Dave enters Bill Johnson's office Dave still not exchanging pleasantries with his boss gets right to the point "Bill I think we desperately need some agents at the show to keep an eye on these Asian men and to keep a look out for the four Arabic men who should be brought in on sight."

"Dave I'd love to send some men to the show but our agents are mostly covering the mayor's luncheon today and this weekend's senators meetings at the Hyatt. I did send six more agents to the hotel for a raid on the Arabic men's room. It should be just about over now." Explains Bill Johnson now a little more apt to listen to Dave's instincts.

Back at the motel the four would be terrorists are led down the elevator to the fourth floor by their Saudi leader Ahmad. Once they reach the fourth floor the men get off the elevator and head to the stairs where they walk down to the parking garage where their white van is parked. Earlier in the morning when the hotel is silent two of the men took the same route to the van and lauded the weapons into the back of the van.

The anxious Arabic men drive quietly out of the parking lot just as two black Ford Broncos pull up at the front of the hotel carrying the six FBI agents who are arriving to join the surveillance team in the lobby for the raid on the now empty terrorist's room.

Once inside the hotel the eight agents run up the stairs armed with semi-automatics and run to the fourteenth floor and straight to the Arabic men's room. Using a card key that the hotel manager has provided the agents burst through the door into the room yelling "FBI, hands up in the air." immediate disappointment consumes the agents as they discover the room is empty of men so they switch the plan from arrest to search mode and discover empty boxes of ammunition and some cut pieces of wire on the floor and in the garbage can hidden inside empty boxes of cookies to hide from the maids. The agents immediately call their report into the office.

A surprised Bill Johnson fills Dave in on the information to keep him up to date. Then says "Dave I have to agree with you on this, but unfortunately we don't have any agents available until tomorrow. I will assign a team to the rest of the show at that time.

"Well I hope nothing will happen before then I will ask Angus to keep an eye out for the Arabic men today and have him get a feel for the Asian men at their booth." responds Dave.

"Good idea Dave but please tell Angus to keep a low profile." requests Bill.

"I will Bill but you do realize Angus has been involved in this work for over ten years so I think he knows how to handle these types of situations." replies Dave trying to quash any fear that Bill might have regarding Angus's abilities in this type of operation.

As soon as Dave exits Bill Johnson's office he is confronted by a Pepsi wired Rasheed who says "Dave I couldn't help but over hear you and Mr. Johnson talking. I think I may be able to help. If you send me to the show I can keep an eye on the Asian men at their booth."

"Rasheed you worked all night I think you should probably go home and get some sleep." Replies Dave trying to persuade his friend.

"C'mon Dave I know you need help and all I have to do is watch these two men and besides I've had way too much sugar and caffeine to try and sleep anytime soon." pleads Rasheed looking for an adventure.

"alright Rasheed but remember you're not a field agent so don't make any contact with the men and try not to hang around the booth too much." says Dave giving in to Rasheed's request realizing that since Rasheed had helped out in the previous summer he has become much more interested in expanding his role in the FBI and there really was no way for Dave to stop him from just going on his own. Besides Dave also realizes that having these men watched is very important so giving in to Rasheed he has mixed feelings.

Angus and Jim are once again in the coffee shop having their usual all coffee breakfast when Angus's cell phone rings. He checks the call display number and notices that it's Dave phoning from his FBI office. So Angus excuses himself and walks into the hotel lobby where he answers the phone with "Good morning Dave."

"I hate call display". complains Dave then he adds "We got that report back on the other two Arabic men. One is an Egyptian and little is known about him, other than he entered a week ago and he too is staying just outside of Detroit. But this is where it gets interesting, the other man is a known Syrian man. Meaning he is a known man with terrorist links so he should never been allowed into the country in the first place." reports Dave.

"Great you stop Cat Stevens from entering the country but neglect to prevent a known terrorist from getting in?" Asks Angus his voice dripping with sarcasm.

"Yeah that's about right Angus." says an obviously annoyed Dave then he continues "We raided their hotel room this morning and they had already left. All that was found were a few empty boxes of bullets and some cut pieces of wire. It doesn't look good. We have sent out an all-points bulletin accompanied with the photos to the Chicago police force and are agents as well. Angus we aren't too sure that they were doing anything other than some research of the McCormack center and there is a mayor's gala today and also some senators are in town for meetings. I would feel better though if we also were able to get some agents to that show but management has decided that the other two events are much more likely terror targets."

"Well Dave we have felt that the next series of targets are going to be soft targets that concentrate on civilian casualties like they do in other countries like Indonesia and Iraq." Adds Angus.

"That's my feeling to Angus." agrees Dave who then adds "The surveillance team followed the four Arabic men to a local mosque last night where they saw them talking to two Asian men which they took pictures of. Our office have identified these men as an Indonesian man and a Chinese man. They both have one month working visas and they own a booth at the kitchen and bath show called Pure Ceramics. My bosses here believe that the four Arabic men just met these two men earlier at the show and were just saying hello but like you my instincts don't like coincidences. So on top of having the local police and our agents covering the two political events looking for the four Arabic suspects, I also went behind my boss's backs and sent a man from our research department down to the McCormack center to keep an eye on the two new men at their booth. "Angus, do me a favor and check up on the guy please he's not a field agent but he volunteered for the assignment when he heard the boss turn down my request for men at the show. Also could you check out the Asian men's booth I would feel a little bit better knowing at least that these men know a little about the product they are selling."

"Well Jim I will be leaving for the show in a few minutes. So once I get there I will check out the two booths and take a few looks around for the Arabic men. Can you forward me the pictures of the Oriental men on my cell phone and also on your agent so I can check up on him? Also what is his name?" asks Angus getting a little bit of that adrenaline rush that his old job used to give him.

"Good idea Angus. I'll get the pictures away to you right now and the kids name is Rasheed." Says Dave then he adds "And Angus if you do see the suspects call it in don't try and be a hero you have been out of practice for a few years."

"Oh don't go worrying about that Dave. I stopped trying to be a hero after that bomb in Kabul made scrambled eggs out of my brain." Angus says bye to Dave then heads back to the coffee shop for another coffee with Jim.

In the parking lot at the McCormack center in a white cargo van the six terrorists are meeting. Ahmad the leader says "Allah is with us today, this van was left for us in the underground parking lot by our Armenian friends. Good thing to because it sure looked like two agents sitting in the hotel lobby last night. Those guys want to do stake outs properly then they better get new tailors." Ahmad then takes two boxes and hands them to each of the Asian men adding "Inside these boxes underneath the literature for Pure Ceramics are the back packs loaded with twenty pounds of plastic explosives and twenty pounds of ball bearings like the ones used by our brothers in the attacks in Lebanon. Today will be a great day for the Infada. Ahmad then hands the AK 47's and the money belts packed with plastic explosives back to the Arabic men keeping one of each for himself. Ahmad then looks around the parking lot and notices it is pretty well empty except for a few of the exhibitors who have arrived early to finish up some last minute details in their booth before the show begins and the public is allowed in, in about an hour. Ahmad nods to the Asian men and says "May Allah be waiting for you."

The two Asian men get out of the van and walk towards the building carrying their boxes while the white van pulls away and out of the parking lot. Once inside the McCormack building the Asian men open their boxes and spread the literature around the booth. They then put the boxes with the backpacks still inside into a cabinet that is part of the display.

Outside in the parking lot the local police have arrived to check the vehicles for the four Arabic suspects. The two Asian men also notice that heavy security has arrived at the entrances to check all the bags and packages of the arriving public. The men feel fortunate that there was no security to check the exhibitors as they entered other than to check for their exhibitor passes.

Angus and Jim arrive at the show and have to join the long slow moving line of visitors trying to enter the show. After a half hour they finally reach the entrance where they are searched thoroughly and made to pass through a metal detector. When they get inside Jim says "Well I feel a whole lot safer now with all that security around." Angus not wanting to alarm Jim more than he already has chooses not to mention that the security in Iraq and Afghanistan was always a lot tighter than this but somehow the terrorists usually still found a way to be able to detonate their explosives.

Angus tells Jim "I want to go check out that booth with the faucets for Dave but Jim if you hear or see anything suspicious today just head for the nearest exit and get outside."

When Angus reaches the booth with the faucets he sees only one short plump grey haired man. As Angus introduces himself and shakes the man's hand the man says in a heavy Italian accent "Hello my name is Tony Rosario. I am the owner of this company and I am looking for distributors in North America."

"Where are your men that I saw in the booth yesterday assembling for the show?" asks Angus.

"Oh you must mean my three sons, but you know how young men are these days, they do a little work then stay out all night chasing women then they are too tired in the morning to get up and do some more work again." replies the man.

"Well I don't know about young men but I have an older business associate who definitely belongs to that club." Says Angus with a laugh as he points Jim out to Tony while Jim is standing right beside Angus shaking his head with a smile on his face. Then Angus adds "No Tony I mean the four men who were here yesterday they said this was their booth and they were the distributors for the whole United States."

"I wish I handsome dealers here but I don't that is why I have to work this whole show with only my sons to help." replies Tony. Jim compliments the man on his booth then hands him one of Jim's cards and says "I would be very interested in following up this line if you are also looking for any dealers inside Canada."

Angus then says to Jim as they leave the faucet booth "I also told Dave that I would check out the Pure Ceramics booth for him."

"Now you are starting to scare me again Angus" says Jim as they head off towards the Pure Ceramics booth.

"Don't worry too much Jim remember I was trained to suspect everybody when I worked in anti-terror so it's probably nothing at all." comforts Angus not too successfully.

"Oh great, I feel much better now" responds Jim. Angus and Jim arrive at the Pure Ceramics booth and Angus checks out his cell phone photos of the two Asian men that were seen at the mosque with the four Arabic suspects. Both of the Asian men are working in the booth but before Angus enters the booth he spots a tall thin young man of Indian descent wearing a dark blue suit and wearing sunglasses indoors. Angus chuckles to himself realizing that the man is indeed Rasheed. Angus walks over to the bench Rasheed is sitting in and says "Rasheed I'm Angus Gellar, Dave told me you were coming here to keep an eye on our two friends here. I'm going to ask them a few questions about plumbing then head over for a coffee. Why don't I meet you there and I'll tell you what I have learned."

"Okay Angus I could use a Pepsi I'll wait for you there." answers Rasheed.

Angus enters the Asian men's booth and starts asking questions to determine their knowledge of the product. "Hi my name is Angus Macpherson from Toronto Canada." Angus introduces himself as he slips each of the men his business card. The man look at the card for a moment then one says "Angus just call me Fred." An obvious name that the man has picked up for the show.

"What are the flush rates of your toilets and what colors are they available in?" Asks Angus getting straight to the point.

"All out toilets are CSA approved for Canadian us and UL approved for USA distribution they work on the six liter flush ballcock. Most of what we have is white but we also match the American Standard and Kohler main colors. Especially bone and grey others can also be ordered in runs." Answers the man named Fred.

"What are some of your prices?" Asks Angus now interested in the quality of the product and expecting a low price.

"Our standard drop in basin is six dollars and our regular insulated toilet is twenty two dollars each, the toilets are supplied with wax gaskets and floor bolts and a toilet seat and water supply. All prices are quoted in USA dollars and freight is fob China so a full container costs four thousand to ship. And all payment are to be by letter of credit received before shipping starts." Explains Fred.

Angus nods to Jim to carry on the discussion for the product as Angus slides away towards Rasheed and the coffee bar. Angus orders at all cream only coffee and a large Pepsi on the rocks for Rasheed.

Angus sits beside Rasheed who accepts the Pepsi with a surprised look on his face and Angus says "Dave Gellar forwarded me a picture of you Rasheed and he also told me about your addiction to cola drinks."

"Thanks Angus Dave also told me about your dependency on coffee." replies Rasheed.

"Okay Rasheed these men do know a lot about the material they represent but I think it would still be a good ideate keep a quiet eye on them today at least until more agents can take over tomorrow." Suggests Angus who then adds "Rasheed you may get bored so walk around the show and try not to make eye contact with men and if you have any questions I'll try to circle by every half hour or so. Also here is my cell number call me for anything and maybe lose the sun glasses they are a bit much."

Angus leaves the coffee shop and phones Dave to report in as he wonders through the crowd. "Dave Gellar here," Says Dave as he answers the phone

"Morning Dave Angus here. I checked on the booths the Arabic men were nowhere to be seen and that booth is really run by an Italian man who has his three son's working for him so I think the search for the Arabic men should intensify. On the other hand the two Asian men in the Pure Ceramics booth legitimately know their product. But this doesn't mean that they are just suspects who took their homework seriously. And Dave your man Rasheed could only be more noticeable if he was wearing a badge on his jacket." Dave chuckles and says "Thanks for the update Angus but the bosses can't free up any agents for there until tomorrow and I have to man the search for the four Arabic suspects from back here. So the show is pretty well going to be an unguarded soft spot today other than for you and Rasheed. Do you have a gun Angus?" asks Dave.

"A gun, are you joking Dave I'm Canadian our military hardly has any guns but if something comes up I'm good at improvising."

Angus and Jim continue to walk the floor of the show and at two o'clock Angus's phone rings and his heart skips a beat when he realizes that it's April's voice on the other end of the line. April says "Angus, Susan has just asked me to invite you out to dinner with us tonight so I thought I'd call first and ask before Dave could reach you again and ruin the surprise." Realizing that he goes back to Toronto in two days Angus jumps at the chance to spend more time with April thinking that he better pick up the pace a bit if he hopes to ever see April again after the trip to Chicago. So Angus adds "April I would be honored to escort you to dinner tonight and although I did talk to your brother just an hour ago he never mentioned anything about tonight."

"You two talk an awful lot Angus, is the only reason you go out with me is to get closer to my brother?" jokes April.

"Very funny April what time should I be ready?" asks Angus

"I'll pick you up at the hotel at about five thirty." Informs April as she says bye.

At four o'clock Angus tells Jim "April is picking me up for dinner tonight with her and her brother and sister in law, so I thought I'd head back to the hotel early and grab a quick shower and shave."

"Yeah go ahead I'm going to hang around here and see if there are any after show parties going on. You have fun with that cute little blonde number and I'll see you in the room or tomorrow."

Angus heads outside with a little extra jump in his step and hails a cab to take him back to the hotel to get ready for his date with April. At the hotel Angus showers shaves and dresses in his black suit and his snappy purple tie not wanting to get lectured from the fashion police again, he looks in the mirror and is pleased that an old man like him can actually clean up this well. Angus catches the elevator and heads to the lobby to meet his date.

At the McCormack center it is a quarter to five and the Indonesian terrorist picks up his backpack and straps it on before heading off to a secluded washroom at the other end of the convention center. He notices that the tall thin dark skinned man in the blue suit who has been hovering around the booth all day is getting up to follow him. The Indonesian man scoots at a quickened pace throw the crowds then behind a blue curtain and into a secluded washroom. Rasheed not aware of the suspect's suspicions follows him into the empty washroom. Rasheed is nervous and his hands are beginning to perspire so his choices to walk beside the man and wash his hands. The terrorist ducks into an empty stall and takes off his backpack then removes a twelve inch hunting knife from his jacket. As the

Indonesian terrorist leaves the cubicle he inadvertently bumps into a nervous Rasheed as Rasheed dries his hands. With a dry throat Rasheed blushes and says "Sorry." The terrorist without hesitation grabs Rasheed's forehead with his left hand and with his right hand he slices the knife across Rasheed's throat. A stunned Rasheed stares into his wide eyed reflection in the mirror that is quickly blurred by the blood spurting from Rasheed's neck. Rasheed tries to cry out for help but the knife must have severed his vocal chords because all he manages to get out are a few breathily gasps. The terrorist feeling Rasheed's struggles getting weaker takes the knife and plunges it repeatedly into the dying agent's chest. As Rasheed's lifeless body stops struggling the terrorist drags him from under the arms into an unoccupied stall where the terrorist sits Rasheed's body on the toilet seat and locks the stall. The terrorist then crawls out of the stall underneath the door and washes the blood from his hands and puts away his knife then straps the backpack back on and exit's the washroom and rejoins the crowd on the other side of the blue curtains.

At the expresso bar in the McCormack center the crime bosses from New York, Miami and Chicago are sitting down when Sam Guido the head of the New York syndicate says "Where is this little shithole? These new Russian guys call a meeting then show up late they have no respect for the old guard. He better be offering to back off on our territories or he might wake up swimming in Lake Michigan in the morning." Sam gets up and adds "Damn this prostate I'll go hit the washroom and I'll grab another round of coffees on the way back so if this clown hasn't shown up by then, well I think we should just all get up and leave." The others nod in agreement as Sam heads off towards the washroom followed by his two rather large body guards.

The Indonesian terrorist enters the expresso bar and walks over to his three targets sitting drinking their coffees. He walks right past the intended victims with his breath rapid and shallow and his hands shaking he walks to the counter to take a deep breath and recompose himself. He then gathers his strength and text messages his Chinese partner the codewords *Allah is great* and heads back over to the table where his primary targets are seated, only to be disappointed that only two of his targets are still sitting in their places. He decides it is way too late to change his plans now so he walks right up to the table with the Miami and Chicago mob bosses and grabbing the detonator he screams out "DEATH TO AMERICA" as he presses the button. The ensuing blast immediately kills the intended targets as well as another seventy bystanders as well as injuring another hundred more.

In his booth upon receiving his text message the Chinese terrorist grabs his backpack from the cabinet and straps it on while heading for the main entrance to the show.

Jim in the aisle walking hears the loud explosion and startled he remembers Angus's words to head straight to the closest exit. So he quickens his pace and heads to the closest side of the building stumbling upon the mayhem in the coffee hut. Jim's pulse starts to race as he is confronted by pieces of flesh, bone and blood scattered throughout the area. Jim stumbles and drops to a knee as he stepson a bodiless arm in the aisle way. Jim fells panic taking over him as he glances up from the floor and sees a decapitated head of a young man laying a few feet from his hands. Jim hops too his feet and rushes to the red sign saying exit and bursts through the door and runs down the stairs his mind still not yet comprehending all that he has taken in.

In the washroom Sam Guido's body guards react with instinct at the loud blast outside and throw Sam to the ground and cover him with their bodies. Then the burly men jump up and grabbing an arm of Sam's each lift him up from the floor and head out of the washroom and into the mayhem of blood and guts spewed across the blast site. The guards rush Sam out the side emergency doors and onto the street below.

"I never thought this fucking prostate cancer would save my life." Says Sam to nobody in particular.

Meanwhile back at the main entrance of the show The Chinese terrorist is anxiously waiting for the lobby too fill up as the confused mob becomes shoulder to shoulder in the lobby the Chinese terrorist squeezes his way into the middle of the mass of humanity and with a deep breath he screams "ALLAH IS GREAT." And he detonates his explosives sending the shrapnel through the throngs off people fighting to leave. The blast immediately kills another two hundred people and injures seriously another two hundred more.

CHAPTER EIGHTEEN

CHICAGO FRIDAY EVENING APRIL 3RD

At five thirty April shows up at the hotel as a light rain begins to fall from the sky. April skips into the hotel lobby wearing a flowered patterned dress with a white background and has a low cut neck trying desperately to show April's missing cleavage. The dress is hemmed a few inches above her knees and Angus thinks that April looks adorable but doesn't say so realizing that adorable is a bad word to say to a women who is trying to present herself as sexy. April leans in and gently kisses Angus hello then says "I've been meaning to ask Angus, where did you get your name from?"

"Well there are a couple of theories April, my mom is from Scotland and says it is a proud Scottish name meaning strength of character. On the other hand my dad says I was named after a hornless beef cow with short black hair that are from his original hometown of Aberdeen Scotland. I prefer to believe my mother but I fear my dad's theory may be far more likely.

When Angus and April arrive at the restaurant for diner they are greeted by a shocked and somber Dave who says "The bloody Bosses refused to listen to us now I just learned Rasheed has been discovered in a washroom at the McCormack center with his throat slash shed from ear to ear and the Oriental men detonated two bombs at the show. One at the coffee bar and another at the main entrance killing over two hundred people and injuring hundreds more. A shocked and disbelieving Angus says "When did this happen I was just at the show and left at four o'clock." Dave answers Angus shaking his head "It happened just a few minutes ago and we're not sure of the survivors or most of the details yet." In a state of panic Angus walks away from the others and phones Jim on his cell phone. He has a sudden feeling of relief overcome him when he hears Jim's voice on the line saying "I'm okay Angus I took your advice and when I heard the blast I hurried to the nearest exit. But the blood and carnage was incredible it was everywhere and as soon as I got outside I heard another explosion go off. I'm going over to the Mercy hospital now to donate blood and see if any of the casualties are people that we know." Jim shaking takes a breath and adds "You might as well try and enjoy your dinner Angus there's not much more you can do here and I think that will pretty well be the end of the show and we have some time to kill before we leave on Sunday."

When Angus arrives back at the restaurant entrance April greets him with a hug as tears are forming in her eyes. She grabs his hand tightly and asks "Is everything all right with Jim?"

"Well Jim'ds alright yes but we don't know about any of our other friends that were there." answers Angus

"Susan's inside and I think we should head inside to join her t eat besides I don't think anybody at the office is really going to want to see me tonight. Not after all this anyways." says Dave as he leads the others inside to the restaurant where he hugs Susan upon seeing her. Once inside the foursome decide that a good drink before dinner might be the answer to their shakes and so they grab an end table Angus propping his back against the far wall away from the door as to make sure he can see everybody entering and exiting the restaurant. This was a habit that Angus picked up while on duty in Afghanistan. As a prevention for being suckered up by any bombing suspects. Angus takes a quick drink out of his glass and almost chokes as he stops the four Arabic suspects gather inside at the bar. Angus nudges Dave's leg under the table and when Dave looks up Angus nods silently towards the bar and were the four Arabic men are standing. As if on que Susan asks April if she could join her in the washroom to powder her nose. April dutifully accepts knowing the routine of powdering the nose soften accompanied by the women discussing private information about their dates. Well this obvious ruse staking place Dave says to Angus "Let's head to my car for a minute Angus." On their way to Dave's car, Dave phones dispatch and says "Get a stash force down to O'mallets steak and seafood house pronto." The dispatcher responds Sir all of our teams are currently at the McCormack center. But I'll will send the first available team to your location, they should be there in a half hour or so," explains the overstressed dispatcher.

"That's not good enough" barks out an angry Dave as he wishes throwing his phone might relax some of his tension.

"That might not be good enough," Blasts a frustrated Dave into the empty line as he once again is overcome with a desire to throw the phone into Lake Michigan

At the car Dave opens his trunk and Angus sees a large blue suitcase when Dave opens it he reveals a virtual arsenal of hand guns and knives and Dave says "Okay commando boy take your choice." Angus carefully looks over his selection then decides on a 9 mm glock handgun and a twelve inch hunting knife that he checks by running his thumb along the blade. Angus immediately discovers his mistake to the plan when a drop of blood starts to form along his thumb. Dave grabs his favorite gun a.357 magnum and a.38 caliber hand gun as back up. Dave and Angus conceal their new found weapons and head back inside casually to their table to await the return of their dates. When Angus notices April and Susan returning from the washroom he spots two of the terrorists that have now moved to the other side of the bar while their two accomplices remain on the side of the bar where Angus and Dave are sitting. As April and Susan sit down Angus wipes the perspiration from his upper lip with the hankie the bar has supplied. Angus says "Okay ladies now it's my turn to check out the plumbing. Angus nods to Dave that he is going to get closer to the other two men at the far side of the bar thereby leaving the two closer men for Dave to watch.

When Angus arrives at the far side of the bar he notices that one of the men is leaning against the bar with his leg unknowingly shaking with nerve, the other man is standing about thirty feet down in front of a table consisting of four seated men three are of Japanese decedent while the fourth is a Caucasian of eastern European features. Angus decides to position himself next to the man leaning at the bar and grabs hold of the twelve inch knife that he has in his belt with his right hand while gripping the gun with his left hand. At the same time the front door springs open with the laughter of six families of Jewish descent who have just exited the synagogue across the street they are followed in by numerous patrons who welcome the smells of the restaurant and the warmth inside the building.

The Caucasian man stands in the sudden confusion endmost the Arabic terrorist nearby as he heads off towards the washroom. Angus sees the signal that the Caucasian man has made and takes it as a signal to the start of the events so he clasps the knife tightly in his hand. The Arabic man standing near the Japanese men at the table reaches under his coat and draws out an automatic machine gun opening fire on the unsuspecting Japanese men killing them instantly. Angus reacting with instincts only pulls out his hunting knife and thrusts its sharp blade into the shocked terrorist's throat. The blade slides through the esophagus and through the spinal cord paralyzing him instantly. So, the bleeding suspect slides to the floor Angus quickly draws out his lock 9 mm gun from his pocket and fires two rapid rounds at the machine gun toting Arab, the first enters through the right eye on its way into the terrorists brain the second bullet follows the same path with one exception it enters the left eye on its path towards the brain. The terrorist's falls face first to the floor with blood streaming from his eyes and he can no longer get off any more rounds of fire as he crumples to the ground dead.

At the other side of the bar upon hearing the bursts of gunfire Dave moves like a cat throwing April and Susan to the floor and then while grabbing his.357 magnum he himself sprawls to the ground his gun aimed at the two Arabic terrorists that he has been watching. Dave without waiting for the terrorists to get the jump on him fires three quick shots the first hits one terrorist between the eyes. Dave second and third blasts find their way into the second terrorist's chest but not before he is able to fire off a single burst from his automatic weapon spraying the latest Jewish family who has entered the restaurant wounding three of the children. Dave fires a fourth shot into the left side of the head of the terrorist as the man falls to the ground gasping from his chest wounds tearing away half of the terrorists scalp exposing the grey matter of his bleeding brain to the air.

With screams and panic permeating in the bar Angus spots the Caucasian man who was sitting with the Japanese men trying to sneak out the side door under the blanket of confusion that engulfs the bar. In his loudest voice Angus screams "Freeze FBI" as he aims his gun at the suspect's face, the man drops to the ground on his knees with his hands clasped behind his head. Angus hollers "Dave come here quickly, I need your handcuffs." Dave arrives in a run and hands Angus his cuffs and Angus firmly cuffs the suspect's hands behind his back. Dave rushes over to the two dead men that Angus had taken down earlier and rolls the men onto their backs. As he does Dave notices that both men are wearing heavy money belts with wires sticking out so Dave flashing his FBI badge yells at the bar patrons "Everybody outside quickly until we secure the bar and restaurant." The crowd doesn't have to be coaxed a second time as they make their way outside into the rain. Dave then walks over to the bar manager and says "You better get your people outside also and try to keep as much calm as you can out there until we get some backup here."

"Who's going to pay all the customers' bills?" Asks the shaken manager. Angus in disbelief sits. "Just be glad you're still alive these men meant to kill everybody in here tonight." Angus walks over to the other side of the bar where he sees April and Susan laying on the floor in shock but seemingly unhurt. Angus runs over to the women and when she sees Angus approaching April leaps to her feet and hugs Angus as hard as she can. Dave after checking and making sure all four of the terrorist's are dead calls for the bomb squad and some backup. Angus sees the handcuffed suspect crawling in the confusion in an attempt to get out the door so Angus cracks the back of his gun across the back of the escaping man's head causing him to fall to the ground headfirst as his head starts to bleed. Angus places his right knee into the back of the man's neck and says in a firm voice "I'm going to walk back to the other side of the bar to grab the keys to these cuffs and if you move again I will happily shoot you." As Angus gets up he kicks the man hard in the ribs and yells "You son of a bitch you just bled all over my suit pants." As Angus walks over to Dave to get the keys he sees the persistent suspect jump to his feet and try for one last attempt at escape to the door. So Angus fires a shot through the back of the man's right knee dropping him to the ground again screaming in pain and panic. Angus now wearing a sadistic grin on his face walks back to the man and asks "What did you think? That I was bluffing? I've already killed two of your partners it won't bother me in the least if I kill you also. The man tries to look surprised and through his pain mutters out "I didn't know those men." Angus takes his right foot and steps onto the bullet wound in the back of the suspect's leg. And says "I'm not an idiot. Psychotic maybe but not an idiot, I saw you signal those men as you got up to go to the washroom before they opened fire." The man looks away sheepishly as he realizes he has been caught.

So, the bomb squad and backup team arrive Dave walks over to Susan and kisses her and gives her a reassuring hug. While April whines "Dave you hurt my neck throwing me to the floor." Dave looks at April in shock and realizes she is joking so he quickly hugs his little sister also. Susan grabs the car keys from Dave's pocket and says "I'll drive April back to our house and grab a glass of wine as you guys finish up here but try not to be too long Dave I'm getting hungry." As April and Susan leave the restaurant April rushes over to Angus one more time and hugs him tight again. Angus says "April you're going to break my ribs if you don't ease up a bit." Angus kisses April quickly then April runs out the door to catch up to Susan in anticipation of the nerve calming glass of wine that awaits her.

Dave and Angus grab a ride back to the FBI headquarters with a Chicago police cruiser.

At the FBI headquarters Bill Johnson is waiting for Dave's arrival. Angus and Dave enter and Bill says "I think it's better if I debrief you alone first Dave." Angus grabs a cup of coffee and waits in the lobby for Dave to finish. "How did you know about the threat at the restaurant? And how did you manage to kill four men and capture a fifth with so little collateral damage?" asks Bill.

"Well the man you so rudely kicked out was Angus Macpherson the Canadian anti-terrorist expert I was telling you about earlier. He took down two of the terrorists and captured the other. As for knowing about the attack at the restaurant, well I'm not that good Angus and I were just having dinner with Susan and April there when the four suspects we have been looking for all day just happened to come into the restaurant. I called for backup immediately and was told that something had happened at the McCormack center earlier and nobody could arrive for about a half hour. So Angus and I tried to keep an eye on the men until help arrived." Explains Dave who then asks "The real question you're going to have to answer Bill is why after we lost those men we didn't have the other two men staked out at the show?"

"A good question Dave." Says Simon Lang the federal director at the FBI's counter terrorism office in Washington D C.

"Simon you should have called I would have had somebody pick you up at the airport." says an off guard Bill Johnson.

"I wanted to find out for myself why nobody was watching the show. Then I heard that a researcher was found dead in a washroom at the show. Just what the hell is going on in this office Bill? It seems to me that somebody had suspicions of this attack earlier but somewhere down the line communications broke down and disaster happened so I thought I'd get down here myself and do the debriefing in person and open up an investigation before somebody outside catches on to the fact that we got caught with our pants down. I also want to figure out why a decorated agent like Dave Gellar who had just stopped a major terror attack last summer was according to your reports not the least bit suspicious of anything happening then somehow he shows up and stops a second attack today at the restaurant? So, if you don't mind Bill I would like to take Agent Gellar here and interview him in private." Dave and Simon leave a nervous and perspiring Bill Johnson alone in his office to worry on his own.

Dave sits down in a private room with Simon Lang who says "Okay Dave, Just listen for a minute. I know this office has been having some internal problems for the last few years but I foolishly believed after nine eleven and the summer here that everyone would start to work together. So let me see if I'm right about my theory. I believe you had some strong suspicions about the terrorists. This I know from the research department who you gave the orders to check on seven men. Six of whom are the dead terrorists at the

McCormack center and the restaurant. The last I was surprised to see sitting unguarded in the lobby outside here tonight when I arrived. How am I doing so far?"

Dave knowing in a debriefing the best policy is to always give up all information even if he thinks some of it to be impertinent says "Pretty good so far I'm impressed but the last man, the one in the lobby is Angus MacPherson and I ran a check on him when my sister started showing some romantic interest in him this week." Replies Dave.

"Now I'm guessing again. I presume this is where you found out about Angus's experience in the Canadian anti-terror unit? And figured he had some official involvement here?" asks Simon.

"Yes and no. no I didn't think he was on official business because he is no longer on active duty but yes I did take his instincts very seriously. So at the restaurant after being turned down for immediate backup I took it upon myself to arm Angus and have the two of us watch the suspects until the office finally got around to sending over the extra help." answers Dave.

"Well then get Angus in here I would also like to ask him a few questions." requests Simon Lang.

Dave walks back through the office and calls for Angus to join him. Dave glances to Bill Johnson's office and takes a sadistic pleasure in seeing Bill so visibly upset. Once back inside the room with Simon Dave and Angus sit down as Simon starts "Well Angus it's a pleasure to meet you. I read your bio on the plane on the way over and it's quite impressive. I should also let you know I will be removing your name from our terrorist watch list. Angus looks up at Simon with a puzzled expression and Simon continues with a chuckle "Yeah I had your name put on the list after finding out Agent Gellar ran a security check on you the same week as he ran the checks on the six dead terrorists. I would like a written report from the both of you on the week's events in the morning and Dave you are now directly under my command and reporting to me from now on and not Bill Johnson. I would also like to remind you that from now on only field agents do surveillance duties and you won't be denied that request again" Dave looks at Simon questioningly so Simon continues "Yeah Dave you have been promoted and that part about the field agent surveillance was just a guess and I can see by your shocked reaction that I'm right." Finishes Simon.

Angus and Dave sit quietly for a minute before Simon starts "We are trying to connect why the syndicate bosses from New York, Miami and Chicago were meeting at the home show. We also see that on the security tapes from the Mccormack center that the first bomber went out of his way deliberately to detonate his bomb beside the table where the mob bosses were meeting. We picked up Sam Guido of New York an hour ago under the suspicion that he may have been behind the hit on the other two leaders because he had just left the table a moment before the bomb exploded but Sam said the three of them were all called there to meet with a representative of the Russian mob who was in town from Toronto but he failed to show up. It's also quite a coincidence that the man you apprehended at the restaurant is an Armenian member off the Russian syndicate out of Miami." Simon drinks down the rest of his cold stale coffee and gags like he is about to throw up before he continues "The Japanese men that were killed at the restaurant were members of the Yukussa in charge of the brothel business in Thailand and Taiwan. These are a little too much of a coincidence for me so Dave your first assignment while working for me is to find out how all these coincidences connect together." Simon stands up and opens the door and says "I'll meet you back here on Monday morning Dave and we will gather a new task force to try and figure out answers to these questions. And Angus thanks for your help. If Bill Johnson wasn't so busy looking over his shoulder worrying that another agent might replace him we might have ben able to prevent both of the attacks today but as it stands over a hundred people in that restaurant owe their lives to you and Dave and your quick reaction."

Dave and Angus grab a cab back to Dave and Susan's house. When they enter the house Dave notices two bottles of red wine sitting on the dining room table, one is empty and the other is well on the way to joining it's partner in the recycle bin. Angus enters the kitchen where April and Susan are laughing. Angus is about to make a sarcastic comment about the wine when his breath is taken away by April who is wearing a backless black dress that is hemmed eight inches above her knees. She has her blond hair pulled back accentuating her beautiful long neck and is wearing four inch spiked black heeled shoes that show off her shapely legs. April rushes over to greet Angus and grabs his hand. Angus's slightly inebriated girlfriend says "Susan got her mother to spend the night minding the boys while we go out to dinner, and Susan decided to get two rooms for the night at the Marriot.

"Why do they each want a room?" asks Angus with a dry smirk on his face and as he finishes his sarcastic comment April playfully elbows him in the ribs replying, "Are you really that slow Angus Macpherson or are you just being a jackass?"

"I'l take the latter it seems like the safer choice." answers Angus.

The women start to feel the buzz from the wine as the adrenaline rush they received from the action at the restaurant starts to wear off. Stuart and Etan come running into the kitchen excited to see their dad and Stuart says "Dad you're on CNN and they are saying that you are a hero for saving a lot of people at a restaurant."

"What are you doing watching CNN Stuart? You are fourteen you should be watching sports or Star trek something like that at your age. Angus watches the news and there is no report of him other than the mention of another unknown agent that helped Dave Gellar.

The two men and the two overdressed a tipsy women get in the car and Dave drives to the Marriot hotel. Susan suggests "Why don't we eat in the steak house here April says that it was good the other night and that ways you boys can have a drink and relax without having to worry about driving. I think April and I are well beyond the stage of being able to drive already."

"Twist my rubber arm." says Dave happily knowing that he can just relax after dinner and head up to the room with his wife without having the fear of locking the door or else having the children come bursting in on him at an awkward moment.

"Who knows without the boys we might even have time for foreplay honey." Says Susan while winking at her husband.

"You Canadians know what foreplay is don't you Angus?" jokes April trying to embarrass Angus.

"Of course, we do April it's a six pack of Molson dry and a slap on your butt." counters Angus who then adds "Actually honey I'm so good at foreplay with me it's been renamed six play."

"Oooowwww, increased expectations." Exclaims April.

The two couples arrive at the Marriot hotel Steak house and notice a huge crowd gathered around the bar watching the television that is playing the news from CNN. A man who has been watching the news and is on his fifth scotch sees Dave walking into the bar area from the lobby and shouts to anybody that happens to be around and will listen "Look there's that cop who stopped those bastards in the restaurant!" Angus looks around the bar and sees Dave trying to shrink awat out of view but it's already too late as a mob rushes over to meet Dave. April and Susan meekly shift away from the gathering crowd swarming Dave but take enjoyment in watching Dave in obvious discomfort from his new born fame. Angus decides that Dave may try to shift the crowd's attention by implicating him so he chooses to join the women in their secluded spot.

Angus finally takes pity on Dave or he is too hungry to wait any longer so he heads over to the restaurant manager and says "Excuse me, but would you please get us a table for four in a secluded part of the dining room. My friend seems to be under siege at your bar" The manager rushes over to the bar and grabs Dave by the arm saying loudly "Leave this man alone he is hungry. Being a hero is hard work." A thankful Dave joins April, Angus and his wife at the table and sits down to grab his breath saying "I don't know how Michael Jordan survived in this town so. It must have been horrible to have been mobbed every day."

"He stops one attack and he's comparing himself to the greatest player ever." says April teasing her brother.

"Yeah Susan I hope a big ego doesn't run in the Gellar family, eh." Says Angus to a chorus of laughter at his Canadian use of the word eh.

"Oh believe me Angus it gets much worse with the women in that family." replies Susan

As the verbal sparring comes to a stop the restaurant manager reemerges with a waiter who is holding a camara. The manager asks Dave in a voice with a heavy Greek accent "Sir would you mind us taking a picture of you shaking my hand for our wall of fame at the bar?" Dave agrees and after the picture is taken Angus asks sarcastically "Oh Dave would you please do the honors of signing my napkin?"

"Okay that's enough, let's eat." Responds Dave now getting upset and not enjoying the constant barrage of jokes any longer. After the four finish their free dinners of Greek salad Steak and shrimp and a Spanish coffee, The Manager returns to escort the two couples out a side exit that leads directly into the hotel lobby next to the elevators. The secret escape has worked as nobody spots Dave leaving. April asks Anus "Aren't you just a little bit disappointed that you weren't reported as a hero along with Dave?"

"God no, I got over being recognized in public back in my college days playing football at Syracuse. Answer Angus truthfully then he adds "I'm just happy to be a part of Dave Gellar's entourage." says Angus with a laugh. On the way up the elevator Dave breaks the silence with "There was a lot more to those terrorist attacks than meets the eye. April would you mind if Angus had a coffee with me back downstairs so that I can bounce a few of my thoughts off him?"

"Oh Dave yes I do mind. Somehow I get the impression with you two that it doesn't really matter what I say. So just don't be too long. Okay?" In response to April's word Angus takes her by the hands and kisses her gently and says "Just one coffee honey then I'll be right up." On their way to the coffee shop Angus and Dave are relieved to see that the crowd at the bar has dissipated so they continue uninterrupted in the coffee shop where Dave orders two coffees and Angus asks "Did you really have some theories to bounce off of me or is this just a ruse to keep my hands off your little sister?"

"No really Angus I get a strong vibe that there is a connection between the terror attacks and the Russian crime syndicate."

"Duh. Yeah Dave It will up to your guys to make that prisoner we caught talk soon or I will bet that there are more plans in the works already. We found out in Afghanistan that there was usually a tapestry of plans in the works. Whenever we stopped one we knew we just had to increase our surveillance teams because more attacks were to follow usually sooner rather than later." Angus says the gulps down the rest of his lukewarm coffee as he adds, "Can we get back to our rooms now Dave I'm tired."

"Yeah sure you are tired. Just remember that April is still my little sister and try not to act so excited to get back to her." Responds Dave as he gets up and heads over with Angus towards the elevators.

Angus opens the door to his room with his heart racing with anticipation of April's touch. When he notices that all the lights are out except the one lamp that is on the night table on what is obviously been picked to be his side as April has claimed the other side of the bed already laying there. As he approaches the bed Angus sees that April is laying on her back in a dark blue satin teddy. Angus notices that the dark blue color of the material makes a striking contrast to April's creamy white thighs and her golden blond hair. Angus takes off his suit and hangs it up quietly. Then he walks back to the bed and sees Aril's chest heaving with each breath. As he reaches the bed Angus is filled with disappointment when he hears a slight snore escape from April. Realizing that tonight is not the night as planned Angus takes the comforter and blanket from his side of the bed and gently folds it over his sleeping beauty. He then puts on his Syracuse sweatshirt to keep him warm seeing he just used his covers to cover April. Angus then crawls gently into the bed and kisses April on her forehead half hoping that like the real sleeping beauty she will to awaken with a kiss but alas Angus is not a prince so April's slumber continues. Angus decides to sit there and watch his new found love sleep and just drinks up her beauty before the day's actions overtake him and he falls into a deep slumber himself.

CHAPTER NINETEEN

DAY 5 IN CHICAGO SATURDAY APRIL 4TH

Angus wakes up first and quietly grabs a shower without waking up April. Angus dresses in the washroom and when he comes out April is awake and curled up inside the blankets. Then she stretches and gives a big yawn. Then April moans "Angus, why did you let me drink so much wine last night?"

"I didn't have much of a say in it April. You and Susan were well on your way to hangover morning before Dave and I got back to the house." Says Angus trying to absolve himself of all blame. The phone rings and April answers "Yeah Dave what do you want?"

"Geez April, not a good night last night? Wasn't Angus up to the task?" asks Dave jokingly because he had received the same reception when he returned to his room.

"No Dave I was asleep before he got back here. But he stuck around anyway so I guess there is still some hope." Replies April.

"Don't worry April, Susan gave me the same reception and if Angus was half as tired as me he was probably partly happy just to go to sleep also. I called because Susan and I are heading down to the coffee shop for Saturday brunch. So why don't you and Angus meet us there when you're mobile again?" asks Dave

April says to Angus "I'm going to grab a shower and if I'm not out within the hour it probably means that I've drowned in there. But assuming that I survive the shower Dave just invited us for brunch with them in the coffee shop."

While April is in the shower getting her blood circulating again, Angus watches CNN news and most of the morning coverage is about the two terror attacks in Chicago. Angus is pleased to note that Dave is still the only one being identified as to the men that thwarted the terror attack in the restaurant.

April returns from the shower wearing a pair of jeans that our so tight that Angus can't believe she was able to fit into them by herself. She is also wearing a white tee shirt with the Milwaukee Bucks logo on it. April runs over to the edge of the bed where Angus lays and launches herself at him curling up into his body and letting out a cooing noise.

Angus runs his finger through April's damp hair and says "We better get downstairs honey begore Dave eats up the whole buffet." As they head downstairs to the coffeeshop April fits her left hand into Angus's back pocket. When they arrive at the table Dave and Susan are already finishing their second plate and Susan says "It's the early bird that gets the Belgian waffles."

"Ooooooooo, Belgian waffles with fresh fruit toppings c'mon Angus let's hurry." Says April enthusiastically.

"Nice recovery. Hangover gone? Asks Angus under his breath so that only April hears his mutter.

"A shower and a sugar rush like waffles and I can recover from anything." says April.

Angus watches in dismay as April loads up her plate with waffles, scrambled eggs, bacon and sausage. Meanwhile Angus just grabs a coffee and a fresh plate of fruit. Back at the table Angus says "April I didn't think it was possible but those big green eyes even got bigger when you saw the waffles. "Dave laughs and adds "We have to drive Susan's mom home tonight so we and the boys will probably spend the night there. So April why do't you cook one of your Italian dinners for Angus tonight and mind the house until we get home tomorrow around noon?" Susan adds, "Yeah Angus her cooking is almost edible." April flashes Angus a sexy come on look that makes his heart leap into his throat. Seeing April and Angus's reactions to Dave suggestion Susan says "Good it's settled then it's a plan you guys can have the house alone tonight." Davelooks at Angus's plate of fruit and asks "Is that all you are going to eat Angus?"

"With all the food I've eaten this week and no exercise I don't want to blimp out." answers Angus.

"Well if you two had finished your coffee a little faster last night April and I would have given you all of the exercise your bodies could have handled."

In Toronto the Russian syndicate leaders are meeting at Ivan Yuskavich's house, drinking shots of vodka in celebration of the elimination of their major competitors at the terror attacks in Chicago. Ivan says "With the elimination of the crime boss from Miami we can now take over the cocaine traffic from Columbia and the Chicago opening will allow us to take over control of that city as well as the central states and the main drug distribution center from the northeast to the northwest states. Killing the Yususa men at the restaurant means or men have already taken over control of the brothels in Taiwan and Thailand." Valeri Yashin butts in "This operation should have been under our control all along considering we supply the girls from kidnappings in the former east bloc countries and deliver them to the Orient so we were taking all the risks and weren't receiving our just rewards." Ivan starts again "The only set back was the untimely escape of New York's Sam Guido and our secondary plan will put an end to him as well as destabilize the whole countries economy as well as that of the whole western world allowing our country to once again state claim to the role of world's super power. As well the ensuing panic will cause the whole country of the arrogant and squeamish to panic and go into depression for it has never been under adversary or invasion on it's own soil, and with the power shift and depression our drug sales should increase dramatically."

Back at the hotel Angus informs Jim that he is going to be spending the night over at April's but will be home in time for their drive back to Toronto on Sunday.

Angus takes a cab over to Dave and Susan's house in the north end of Chicago. The weather is still unseasonably brisk and windy. Angus knocks at the door and April answers it dressed in her painted on faded blue jeans. When Angus enters the house he is hit with the pleasant aroma of dinner cooking away in the kitchen. April asks "What would you like to drink?"

"A beer please." is his answer then he adds "What's for dinner? It sure smells good."

"I'm baking cannelloni stuffed with spicy sausage, onion, peppers and good old Wisconsin cheese. Answers April as she returns with a frosty mug of beer. Which she places on the coffee table in front of Angus. April sits on the couch beside Angus and places her hand on his knee. April then grabs the television remote and turns on the tube to a Syracuse basketball game versus Villanova. Angus kisses April and says "My, aren't you the perfect woman or what?"

"Let's see what you think after you eat my cannelloni and Caesar salad." Replies April.

"Is there anything I can do to help?" Asks Angus as Syracuse ties the game.

"No watch your game and dinner will be ready in an hour or so." answers April.

April calls Angus into the dining room just as the Orangemen hit a pair of free throws to ice the victory. The table is set with the good china and crystal wine glasses that are filled fill red wine. Angus is ordered to sit-down so he obliges his hostess as she fills the chilled salad bowls with the Ceasar salad. Angus and April eat their dinners with a little conversation and a lot of eye contact. Afterwards Angus clears the table as April loads the dishwasher. April disappears up the stairs. Then after a few minutes she calls to Angus "Angus can you come up here and give me a hand?" Angus rushes up the stairs and to a bedroom where he sees April laying on her stomach in a light blue satin teddy similar to the one she wore the night before. Angus says "Yes ma'am how may I be of service?"

"Can you rub my neck? I think I hurt it a bit last night when Dave threw me on the floor." Asks April determined that tonight she will take control of the situation.

"Yeah it would have been much better if he let you get shot." answers Angus sarcastically trying to use humor inappropriately as a cover for his excitement and nervousness. Angus straddles himself on top of April and starts rubbing her neck. Angus has developed a knack for finding the exact sore spot while giving a massage and being able to work it out quickly. When Angus can feel the tension leaving April's muscles he changes his now full back massage to a light tickling scratch. This meets with April's approval as she starts purring. April rolls over onto her back looking up at Angus who is now straddling April's front and rubbing her slender yet well-toned arms. April still taking charge starts to unbutton Angus's shirt. Stealing a line from The Graduate Angus says "Why miss Gellar, are you trying to seduce me?"

"Angus, there is a time for humor and this definitely is not one of those times." replies April who's breathing has increased substantially. Angus then helps April remove his shirt completely and together Angus and April start taking each other's clothes off acting in a frenzy. They make love until three in the morning then fall asleep exhausted in each other's arms.

In the morning Angus awakens first but instead of rushing into the shower like he always did with his ex-wife. Angus instead just lays there drinking up April's beauty with his eyes. April wakes up, rolls over and looks at Angus and says "Angus I must compliment you on your stamina and also on your, what did you call it? Six play." April grabs Angus by the hand and pulls him out of bed saying "Let's grab a shower then I'll drive you back to your hotel." They get dressed then head out to April's car. The day is sunny but windy and still unseasonably cold. While driving back to the hotel April asks "Angus next weekend is Easter weekend and if you want me I would love to fly up to Toronto and visit you for the holiday. I can fly out on Thursday and get a return flight home on Easter Monday." Angus once again is thrilled that April has once again taken the initiative says "If you can make it up April I will show you a weekend that you will never forget."

When they arrive at the Marriot, Jim is waiting outside having a cigarette leaning against the wall with his bags packed beside him. Angus gets out of April'scar and Jim says "I packed your bag Angus. I thought you two love birds would be a lot later."

April gets out of the driver's side and says "Hi Jim we've decided that I'll come up next weekend and visit your city." Jim leaves to get his car and to give April and Angus some privacy for their good byes. Angus holds April's hands and kisses her before saying "I hate saying good bye April but at least it is for only four days." Angus kisses April passionately again as Jim pulls his car up to the front near Angus and April. Angus goes to get in the car but hesitates and looks back at April and says "April Gellar I think I'm falling in love with you."

"You better mister. I love you to Angus Macpherson."

Angus finally gets in Jim's car and Jim pulls away as Angus turns his head around so that he can keep eye contact with April for as long as he can. Jim smiles at Angus and says "Well Angus my mission on this trip was to get you laid. Not only did we achieve our mission but my dear boy I think you've fallen in love. Very cute girl Angus, good job."

"Yes she is Jim and yes I am in love with her let's go get home."

CHAPTER TWENTY

MONDAY APRIL 6ᵀᴴ

Dave receives a phone call early in the morning from his new boss Simon Lang. Susan rolls over and groans "I hope that new boss of yours doesn't make a habit off phoning you at six in the morning."

"No he just wants me to get to the airport and fly to New York for a meeting but I'll fly back home tonight."

Dave arrives in New York at a little after eleven. He heads immediately over to the New York FBI office at 26 Federal plaza where he heads up to the office where he meets Jack Robinson the head of New York City's anti-terror division the largest anti-terror unit in the country. Jack walks to Dave and shakes his hand enthusiastically and says "You must be Dave Gellar I've heard a lot of good things about you. The reason you are here is because Sam Guido has gathered some information that might be useful to us and he wants to meet quietly with an out of town agent so that he isn't spotted talking to us. Simon and I figured that seeing it has some connection with the attacks in Chicago that you would be the best person to see him seeing you are the best informed agent about all that went on up there." Jack pauses then continues "The meeting has been scheduled for two this afternoon at the Central park café. Try to use some of the time between now and two to buy a pair of jeans and a sweat shirt. That suit screams FBI."

Dave grabs an I love New York sweatshirt off a street vendor but decides to wear his suit pants anyway. He then grabs a cab to the café. Sam Guido is already waiting inside when Dave arrives. Sam is sitting in the corner table drinking a glass of white wine. Dave saunters over and introduces himself "Hello my name is Dave Gellar I was also in the middle of all the action in Chicago.

"Yeah I recognize you from the news. I hope nobody else does. I figured I'm at the stage in my life where I should help my country where I can." says Sam.

"Oh just like Lucky Luciano did during the second world war." adds Dave.

"Something like that, anyways the point is we were summoned to Chicago under the pretense that Ivan Yuskavich the leader of the North American Russian operations was going to meet us at the show to discuss trying to form a better relationship with us. But the bastards were just setting us up. Why did they hire terrorists to do so much damage?" after a short pause Sam answers his own question "I guess they figured that nobody would survive to implicate them in the attacks. We tracked down Ivan Yushavich's whereabouts during last week and it turns out that not only did he never leave Toronto but the local leaders of their operations in New York Chicago and Miami were all in Toronto meeting him."

"Thanks for the information Sam." Thanks Dave as he finishes off his cappuccino then continues "If you think of anything else here is my card don't hesitate to call me that is my own cell phone number. Even the smallest detail to you might help us piece the whole puzzle together."

CHAPTER TWENTY ONE

APRIL 6TH
ALONG THE AFGHAN PAKISTAN BORDER

John Gagnon Angus's former commanding officer is leading a patrol near the Afghan Pakistan border. The patrol consists of two American Green beret officers, two British SAS officers and another Canadian Joint task force two member as well as John. All the men are expert marksmen. As the evening sets in the patrol puts on their night goggles. A half hour later the patrol spots a group of nine men to the west but the sun is too strong for them to make a proper identification of the men so they decide to get a closer look. When the sun has finally set the patrol is within five hundred yards. The patrol is able to get a good look now and determine that the men are armed and the formation reveals that three men in the middle are being guarded by the other six men with three flanked on either side. John looks through his field glasses and concentrating on the three men in the middle, he identifies one as an unfriendly Afghan drug lord. The second is a wanted low level member of Al Qeada. John cannot identify the third man. John orders the marksmen to pick out one of the bodyguards each and he labels the last man for himself. They all drop into their sniping positions and on John's command fire simultaneously two headshots into each of the guards dropping them immediately. Then they each fire a final shot into the fallen men to both make sure that they are dead and to emphasize their purpose to the three remaining men. The three remaining men don't resist or try to run they chose to drop to their knees instead and surrender. The captured men are stripped of their weapons, handcuffed and then forced to hike back to the allies' base. Upon interrogation the Al Qeada man reveals that the third man is a Russian so John calls headquarters who arrange for a Russian officer who is visiting the allies' base on an information exchange program to be flown by helicopter to meet John and interrogate the Russian prisoner.

When the Russian officer arrives he immediately identifies the prisoner "That is Alex Trovski one of the most wanted men in Russia. He was a former member of the KGB until they were dispended after the Soviet Union disbanded. He is wanted back home for his part in the coup attempt against former premier Boris Yeltsin. He is now a member of the crime syndicate that operates in Moscow. He is also wanted in the questioning of the disappearance of over a hundred suitcase nuclear bombs that were in the hands of the KGB instead of the army. The Russian officer walks over to the prisoner and quietly whispers something threatening into Alex's ear in Russian. A startled Alex spits at him and yells something back in a terrified voice. John looking for an explanation of what just took place says to the officer "Can I see you in the other room?" The officer nods then follows John into the adjourning room where John asks "What the hell just happened in there?" The officer replies "I just told him that with all the innocent and not so innocent people that the KGB interrogated in the Soviet Union that there will be no shortage of volunteers to try those same tactics against him back home."

"Oh nice, but what did he say to you?" asks John

"He said a few choice Russian words then he blabbed by mistake and I'm quoting him here. I don't know where the other ninety eight bombs are but I do the other two are already in the safe hands of a sleeper cell in the United States. I think it would best if you let us take him back to Russia and see if we can break him into giving us more information. We use much rougher techniques than you do in the west but remember he is a former KGB agent so it may take us a little longer to break him than normal. I wouldn't worry though everybody has their own breaking point and we'll push him quickly towards his."

John heads back to the main base in Kabul, along with the two Russians in the helicopter where he is told to pack a bag because he is on his way to Toronto.

CHAPTER TWENTY TWO

TUESDAY APRIL 7TH IN CHICAGO

Dave arrives home from his New York trip at three in the morning. He tries to gently climb into bed without waking Susan but she awakens anyways and asks, "How was your trip dear?"

"Oh it was alright but it could have been accomplished just as easily over the phone but I guess the informant believes he is important enough to warrant a person to person meeting." complains a tired Dave.

Dave and Susan fall asleep only to be awakened by the phone. Susan answers it and is quite teed off when it turns out to be Dave's boss again. She looks at the clock and her anger grows when she sees that this time it's even earlier than the day before. She nudges Dave

Dave and grumbles "It's your five o'clock wake up, phone call super-agent." Dave takes the phone and says "Hello."

"Dave, its Simon sorry to wake you up again but can you get down here as fast as you can?" asks Simon. Dave gets up and drags his sleepy body. After Dave is partly revived by the shower he returns to the bedroom to kiss his sleepy wife good bye. Susan wakes up and says "Where do you have to go so early now honey?"

"To the office but I don't know what is up yet." answers Dave hoping it isn't something that will drag him away from his family again.

"Well the promotion is great Dave, but not if you are going to be called in early every day like this." complains Susan now realizing that she might as well also get up and shower before the boys decide the make a mess getting their own breakfast.

"I'll call you ads soon as I know what is going on but the boys don't have to get up for another hour so try and grab a little more sleep." replies Dave to Susan's grumbling hoping to sooth her morning hostilities.

Dave arrives at five thirty to the office that Simon is using while he is in Chicago and Simon looks up and comments "Dave you look like shit."

"Thanks boss. Well I got home after three last night then you called at five. Two hours sleep hasn't worked for me since I left university." responds Dave.

"Well don't worry Dave you have an hour to sleep on the plane ride to Toronto. I want you to fly up there immediately and work there for about a week. We have a report that a Canadian officer has returned from Afghanistan with the report of a linkage between the attacks here on Friday and some possible future attacks so I want you to team up with him and see if you two can gather up any more information. One last thing Dave. This trip is very crucial because the intelligence so far has implicated the possible use of a couple of small nuclear bombs." says Simon with some urgency in his voice revealing his state of worry about the way the situation keeps escalating to new heights.

Dave drives to the airport with pangs of guilt as he tries to figure out what to say to Susan about another road trip so early. These feelings of guilt are only made more intense by the fact that Ryan's autism was just seemingly starting to get under control a bit and he always regresses every time his father is a way for a couple of days. Dave phones his wife from the airport and tries in vein to explain the situation hiding the complete story so that he isn't overheard by any eavesdroppers but Susan is obviously upset so all Dave can do is stand and listen to her whine on for five minutes until Dave is mercilessly called away by his boarding call for the flight to Toronto.

Angus is driving in the northwest section of Toronto when he receives a phone call and is pleased when he learns that it is April calling who says "Hi Angus, I just booked my flight to Toronto and will be landing at six o'clock on Thursday evening and I've booked a room at the Bristol hotel. It's supposed to be close to the airport."

"Why aren't you staying at my house? I have plenty of room at my place." asks a surprised and somewhat disappointed Angus.

"I will next time but I thought for this trip that it would be easier for you if I stayed in a hotel. Besides it just means we won't have to make the bed in the morning and you also know how much I love room service and no woman would ever pass up any opportunity for breakfast in bed." explains April to a dumbfounded and perplexed Angus.

"April you are being silly. I've been looking forward to seeing you again since Jim and I left the Marriot parking lot in Chicago." replies Angus still happy to see April but equally befuddled.

"Now Angus Macpherson, don't you start calling me silly, or I'm going to have to use my brown belt training in tae kwon do out on you and give you a butt whipping." says April with a mischievous grin.

"I'm not too sure about that butt whipping April but I'm willing to try a spanking maybe." flirts Angus.

"Angus you know that is not what they mean when they say we have a spanking new relationship." flirts back April with a little bit of humor.

At five in the evening Angus is once again surprised by the ring of his cell phone. This time it is Dave on the phone. "Hi Angus, I'm here in Toronto so I thought I'd call you to see how you are doing and what you are up to tonight." starts off Dave.

"What the hell are you doing here Dave?" asks Angus.

"Other than freezing my butt off you mean Angus?" replies Dave.

"Yeah. It was so tropical in Chicago while I was there. I could barely stand it but at least you have that refreshing brisk wind to cool off the town." says Angus dripping with sarcasm.

"Well I'm really in town to meet a guy on a case tomorrow. He has found out some information in Afghanistan. Maybe you know him Angus, his name is John Gagnon." says Dave.

"Yeah I know him very well Dave. John was my commanding officer and best friend while I was in Afghanistan. If John has any information Dave, you can bet on it being accurate and important, that's for sure. Dave if you aren't meeting John until the morning, then if you like I can grab a pair of tickets from the office for the Raptor, Celtic game tonight." says Angus.

"That would be great Angus. For a minute there I was fearing you were going to say a hockey game." agrees a grateful Dave looking forward to watching a basketball game and catching up with his new friend.

"Hey, what's wrong with hockey anyways Dave?" asks Angus in a typically defensive Canadian way.

"Nothing I guess except the only hockey fan in our family is April. I guess it's because she took figure skating as a kid for ten years and got to watch the teenage boys play some games on the other rink. I guess with her love of hockey back then I should have figured out that she would end up falling for a Canadian. As for me I never learned how to skate." Answers Dave

"Well the game starts at seven o'clock so I'll pick you up at six. Where are you staying Dave? Asks Angus.

"I'm at a place called the Skyline hotel Angus. Do you know where it is?" asks Dave.

"Yeah I grew up and live in Etobicoke Dave. So be ready and we can grab a bite to eat after the game." Suggests Angus

Angus picks Dave up from the lobby at the Skyline hotel at six fifteen and they arrive downtown at the Air Canada Center for the game at ten to seven with only enough time to grab a couple of beers. It's then that Angus realizes how long it has been since he has attended a sporting event when he pays sixteen dollars for the beer. The game heads into overtime with the Raptors squeaking out a victory over Boston by a score of one hundred and eight to one hundred and five.

On the way back to the hotel Angus pulls into a restaurant within eye distance of the hotel called Stripes and says, "This is my favorite sports bar and I think you will find that the food is good and the portions are massive." This appeals to Dave who still hasn't eaten lunch yet so he is famished. During the dinner Angus says "It's strange you called today Dave because your sister called me earlier today saying she will be in town this weekend so if you are still around on Thursday maybe you can surprise her and meet her with me." suggests Angus.

"Yeah I'm sure that would go over real well. She flies in from Milwaukee to have a nice private weekend with you and upon her arrival she will find her brother checking up on her. You haven't been in a relationship for a while have you Angus? Just a word of advice from an old married guy. She has never had a man spoil her before with affection so show her some undivided attention and she will be quite happy. But I would love to see that look on her face if she thought I was going to be hanging around you two and it would also be nice to get a chance to see her and say hello." answers Dave.

Angus drops Dave off at the Skyline hotel and says "Say hi to John for me tomorrow and if you are going to be working together you will find it to be quite an experience. Dave I think you will find that the interrogation restrictions you have placed on you by the F B I's laws don't apply as strictly here to military personnel. Well good luck and give me a call tomorrow to let me know how you did and how John is. I haven't seen him in years." says Angus as he leaves Dave and drives off for his house where his dog is waiting for him probably with her bladder about to explode and wanting to go out for her before bed walk.

CHAPTER TWENTY THREE

WEDNESDAY APRIL 8TH TORONTO

Dave wakes up early in the morning and navigates his way through the streets of a new city and arrives at the R C M P headquarters at eight thirty. Once inside the headquarters, Dave meets John Gagnon. John is a middle aged man in his fifties and gives off a strong aura of strength and confidence. By contrast, Roger White, the man in charge of the branch is five foot seven inches tall and is pushing a portly two hundred and twenty hefty pounds. Roger's hair is a bright white but his voice is strong and authoritative when he says to John and Dave "All right men we have had men outside Ivan Yuskavich's house all morning and two outside The Latvian House restaurant which is where Ivan Yuskavich goes to lunch every day at one. We will be informed when they leave Alex's house as well as how many men are accompanying Alex by the surveillance team outside his house and then we will be informed when they arrive at the Latvian House by the agents staking out the restaurant." informs Roger White.

Dave and John go to the kitchen in the office to grab a coffee and get to know each other when Dave says "I went to the Raptor game last night with an old friend of yours, Angus Macpherson."

"Oh, how is the old bugger doing? The last time I saw him the doctors were saying that Angus would never walk again," asks John.

"Well you know that terrorist attack that I am credited with breaking up in the Chicago restaurant? Well it was Angus who took down two of the four men and he was also the one who tipped me off about the terrorists in the first place. Are all you Canadian military personnel so paranoid? Asks Dave.

"I prefer to call it observant, but I guess when you see such unbridled hatred towards the west with no provocation in the eyes of a terrorist it makes us all a little more cautious. Maybe I've seen one too many young men blows themselves up under the false pretenses that they will be rewarded in the afterlife for their callous murderous attacks. It doesn't seem to matter how many clerics preach that their hatred is immoral all it takes is one tape from Bin Laden and these men seem to stop thinking rationally for themselves. It may turn out to be a long war that we are in for but I think that as the individual freedoms take hold and quality of life starts improving that we will eventually win over the hearts and minds of the people. But what really gives me hope is that for every one radical that I ran into, I also found a hundred people that were just like you and I only wanting to live a happy loving life in which there is plenty of hope for the future for their children." Says John as he finishes off his speech.

"So tell me is Angus out of his wheelchair or did he go all Ironside on those terrorists in Chicago?" asks John.

"No Angus seems to be in perfect health now except he has a slight limp in his left leg. He even took my sister dancing and if he can keep up with heron the dance floor well then he is better than any man that I have met before." Explains Dave.

"That's great because Angus had an uncanny natural instinct to danger which he used to call his spider sense that was correct almost every time. Do you think he might want to get back to work?" asks John.

"Angus is already working for a plumbing company that is why he was in Chicago in the first place." answers Dave.

"One thing I didn't get the chance to tell you is that our Russian prisoner from Kabul is Alex Trovski, who was a liaison between the Russian mobs here in Toronto and Al Qaeda. We also understand that he has been in Toronto visiting Ivan Yuskavich frequently over the last six months. That is why we are going to go arrest Ivan Yuskavich today." explains John.

"We have an informant in New York who says that Ivan Yuskavich is the main man in all of North America." adds Dave.

"That would fit because they know that our laws allow then to operate without wire taps unless a court order is received for the wiretap but at least now we have a new law that permits us to hold a suspected terrorist or a person with terrorist links without having to charge them formally but it doesn't quite go as far as your patriot act goes but it still is a big help up here." John says in agreement with Dave

Roger White calls for Dave and John saying "Ivan Yuskavich and his entourage have just entered the Latvian House restaurant on Queen Street, so get going and there will be four agents waiting there to back you up."

John drives Dave and himself over to the Latvian House and arrive there before the lunch crowd begins to arrive so John sits at the table nearest the door so that he can keep a lookout on the door to observe anyone entering or leaving the restaurant. Dave decides to take a walk around the restaurant to see if he can find where Ivan and his men are seated. When Dave returns he says "They're in the back room off to the right and Ivan is seated with four burly men at his table."

"Well, let's go get them." says John as he gets up and leads the way to the back room. Dave follows John into the semi-private back room where the five men are all eating a bowl of soup and a bottle of vodka sits in the middle of the table and all five men have a tumbler filled with vodka an ice sitting in front of them to drink. Dave heads directly for Ivan and grabs the bowl of Ivan's hot borscht and dumps the scalding soup onto Ivan's lap. Ivan and two of his body guards jump to their feet quickly. Dave gabs an eight inch metal baton from the inside pocket of his trench coat and gripping it tightly he quickly slams the metal baton violently behind the left ears of the Ivan's body guard on Dave's right dropping the man to the floor unconscious as a puddle of blood forms on the floor around the head of the fallen body guard. Dave the thrusts the baton into the second body guard's solar plexus causing the second guard to drop to his knees gasping for air. The two guards that had remained seated reach into their jackets for their guns but are beaten to the draw by John who signals for the four R C M P officers who have entered the restaurant to come into the back room where they take over the cuffing of the four body guards while John bellows to Ivan "Ivan Yuskavich you are under arrest."

"What for?" asks a bewildered Ivan innocently.

"We're still adding to the list Ivan, but we will let you know as soon as Alex Trovski stops singing." says John

Ivan now goes into a shocked quiet as the look on his face is equivalent to that of a football safety as he realizes that the receiver he was covering has given him the slip and is running downfield to the inevitable touchdown.

A silent and shaken Ivan Yuskavich is lead away to the wagon along with his body guards by a team of R C M P officers who have shown up to transport the prisoners to jail. When Dave and John return to the R C M P office Roger White is there waiting for them. Roger looks up then takes a sip from his coffee and says "Ivan is being detained in isolation at the Metro West detention center in Etobicoke under the rules of that new anti-terror law, which means we can hold him indefinitely while we interrogate him thoroughly. I figured that you two deserved first crack at Ivan so you're scheduled to meet him tomorrow morning at seven o'clock. I picked seven because I thought he might be a little less guarded at that time in the morning before he gets a chance to wipe the sleep out of his eyes. So good luck and see if you can make it back here by eleven to give me an update because there are many people in both the States and my bosses here that are quite anxious to get an update and see if you two can get any type of feel for what they might have been planning.

"Roger how about ten tonight and then early in the morning, more like five o'clock. We found in Afghanistan that late at night and early in the morning makes it harder for the prisoner to keep his story straight or to remember in detail what he said in the first interview session. I would also like to be able to use the threat of deportation to Guantanamo Bay on him." says John.

When John and Dave arrive at the Metro West detention center they are directed into a small interrogation room, where I van is sitting at a table with his wrists handcuffed together and his legs cuffed together then a chain that leads form his handcuffs to his leg irons is attached to each of the restraints then to a metal ring that is imbedded into the cool and damp concrete floor. I van has a look that is both annoyed and worried about his situation. If Ivan expected any comfort or sympathy from Dave or John he was wrong because as Dave sits in a chair across the table from an impatient Ivan, John yanks hard on the restraints causing the metal to dig deeper into Ivan's skin.

"It's about time you guys got here I've been waiting here tied up for two hours and I'm not saying anything until I get to talk to my lawyer." says Ivan Yuskavich as his bitterness give him an adrenaline boost causing a misplaced aura of confidence which John subdues immediately by pulling Ivan's chair out from under him causing Ivan to go crashing to the ground. Sensing that his role in this interrogation is going to be that of the good guy Dave gets up and picks up Ivan's chair and helps Ivan to his chair and to sit down. With every step the chains dig deeper into Ivan causing him more discomfort.

As Ivan sits in quiet John pour Ivan a tall glass of cold ice water and places it on the table in front of Ivan just out of Ivan's reach due to the restraints. John then sits on the table in front of Ivan and deliberately spills the cold water all over the crotch of Ivan's pants.

"As for us being late Ivan don't worry tomorrow we will be here on time to see you at about five o'clock in the morning. So by then I hope your attitude has improved as well as my coordination so that I don't spill the morning hot coffee into your lap like that cold ice water." says John as a devilish smirk covers his face causing Ivan to feel a light dread for the first time since the arrest.

"Also as for the charges well we can go over those in the morning but they will definitely evolve around terrorism so that we can hold you indefinitely and limit your time with your lawyer." finishes Dave still smirking.

"Also Ivan I'm here because we have information that involves you with the terror attacks in Chicago and my bosses are pressing me to get you transferred to Guantanamo Bay so that you may be held for years with no outside contact and that we will not have to worry about any foolish laws or rules involving interrogation procedures.

The transfer papers should be delivered as soon as the paper work gets finished. Says Dave threateningly.

"And Ivan we to are cracking down a lot harder on terrorism so you might only get an hour or two with your lawyer before your flight to Gitmo." interjects John as his smirk widens again.

"Ivan the rules here give the Canadians a lot more freedom when dealing with suspected terrorists but nowhere near as flexible as the Patriot act is in the States." reiterates John as he tries to leave Ivan in fear with a lot to think over for the night.

"We'll be back bright and early in the morning tomorrow Ivan so the sooner you come clean with the information we want the more likely that you will be able to avoid that long lonely stay south of the border." finishes John with one more threat to let Ivan stew over.

CHAPTER TWENTY FOUR

THURSDAY APRIL 9TH TORONTO

Valerie Yashin Ivan's lawyer and friend files an appeal at the old city hall court in Toronto at nine in the morning and Valerie is granted full access to interview his client in privacy. Valerie decides to head over and see Ivan at around noon.

John and Dave decide to let Ivan sit in chains waiting again for an hour or so before they arrive with fresh Tim Horton's coffee. John is visibly pissed off and tells Dave "Ivan's lawyer won the right to see him again today and he has scheduled a meeting at noon with his client. Therefore this might be our last talk with Ivan where he will feel totally isolated but any of our interviews with him will take precedent over those of his lawyers so it is more of a nuisance to us rather than a major setback. Besides, we really are working on getting him transferred to Gitmo." finishes John.

When John and Dave enter the interrogation room Dave places a large coffee in front of Ivan in the hopes that this one little gesture will make Ivan take down his defenses and be more cooperative. Ivan looks very tired and distraught.

John sensing that he should get things started says "Well Ivan what do you have to say for yourself today? As for us, we have learned that there is now a big backlash going on in the States and Asia against the Russian gangs that were starting to think of themselves as more important in the criminal world than they actually were. I mean Ivan didn't you expect a big backlash once it came out that you tried to kill off the other gang members to increase your status? I think it will only be a matter of time before the long arm of the others organizations are able to reach inside of here. So maybe your transfer to Guantanamo Bay, although it may be uncomfortable, it will undoubtedly extend your life for a while at least and who knows in twenty years or so when you are an old useless man maybe you will receive parole and the other organizations will have forgotten your involvement in killing their leaders," bluffs John.

John's bluff backfires as Ivan's backbone stiffens and he becomes completely uncooperative and refuses to say anything at all.

Angus drives to Cloverdale Mall in Etobicoke filled with excitement at the thought of April soon being back in his arms. Once he is at the mall Angus picks up a few items to surprise April when she arrives at her room.

Angus arrives at the Bristol place hotel and bribes the concierge with a twenty to let him fix up April's room before she arrives. The concierge says no but he agrees to follow Angus's instructions and set the room up for him. After a brief period of disappointment, Angus agrees.

At noon Ivan Yuskavich is glumly waiting in the dark and dank interrogation room for another unwelcome visitor when he is pleased to find that his visitor is none other ten his friend and lawyer Valerie Yashin. In his glee to see his lawyer friend Ivan rushes out a series of questions. "Tell me what you have found out Valerie. What have they charged me with? Can they really send me to Gitmo as they are threatening to? And do they really have anything connecting us to the Chicago attacks?

"One question at a time Ivan we're in no rush. First, you are charged under Canada's new anti-terror law which means you can be held for an undetermined period of time but I am allowed to visit you anytime and lastly we will fight strenuously to stop any extradition proceedings that they might try. As of now only one suspected terrorist has been handed over to American authorities from Canada and his lawyer wasn't half as good as I am." answers Valerie Yashin.